MY BROTHER'S ENVY II

John L. Rose

Good2Go Publishing

My Brother's Envy 2
Written by J. L. Rose
Cover Design: Davida Baldwin
Typesetter: Mychea
ISBN: 978-1-947340-01-5

Published 2017 by Good2Go Publishing
7311 W. Glass Lane • Laveen, AZ 85339
www.good2gopublishing.com
https://twitter.com/good2gobooks
G2G@good2gopublishing.com
www.facebook.com/good2gopublishing
www.instagram.com/good2gopublishing

Dedications

This book is dedicated to two people. First to God, because of the gift He blessed me with, and then to each of my fans, who have been down since day one when *Tied to a Boss* was first born. I thank and love each of you; because without you all, who would J. L. Rose be?

Love

Acknowledgements

I've got to thank my mother, Ludie A. Rose, because she's the key to the strength that keeps me going when I sometimes feel like I just want to give up. I love you, gorgeous! And to the one person who gave me a chance and is still taking chances with me, Ray Brown. Whether you know it or not, I respect and thank you for everything you're doing for me. As long as I can keep thinking and doing whatever I must to keep representing Good2Go Publishing, I'ma hold down the family, and that's on everything. Thanks, man!

Good2Go 4Life!

MY BROTHER'S ENVY II

PROLOGUE

"I SEE YOU'VE MADE friends," Detective Wright stated as Boss shut the passenger door.

Boss ignored Detective Wright's comments and asked, "Where's this information you told me you got?"

Wright reached over across Boss, opened the glove compartment, and took out a thick brown folder, which he tossed onto Boss's lap.

"Here are Malcolm Warren Jr.'s and his father's records you wanted to see."

"I didn't ask for his father's file," Boss stated while opening the folder and beginning to look through the papers.

"I figured since Malcolm Sr. started the business his son is now running, you would want to know what you're up against once you actually try to go up against Malcolm Jr.," Detective Wright explained to Boss.

Boss listened to what the detective told him as he read through the paperwork on Malcolm Jr. He then turned the page and continued reading, but froze after reading something that caused a small smile to spread across his lips.

"Ain't this some shit!"

"What's that?" Wright asked, staring at Boss and seeing

the smile on his face.

"It's just a small world!" Boss said as he closed the folder. "I'ma have a little something extra for this in your payment this Friday."

Boss climbed out of the SUV and walked back around to the sidewalk where Trigger and the others stood waiting for him. Boss then stopped in front of his team.

"What did your rat have to say?" Trigger asked.

"He just brought me something I asked for," Boss answered, holding up the folder. "I'ma have some new shit for the team tomorrow, so I'ma want everybody on point and ready early tomorrow."

"What's up now, nigga?" Eazy asked Boss.

"I need to handle something real quick, but put Butter, Joker, and Black Widow in the three lieutenant spots, and have Butter and Joker at the meeting tomorrow."

Boss dapped up with the team, and then he and Trigger walked off and headed to Trigger's truck. Boss got in the passenger side while Trigger got behind the wheel.

"Big bruh, what's the deal?" Trigger asked as he started up the truck and began driving off.

"You remember shorty I told you about who I met at the gas station in the Porsche SUV?" Boss reminded him. "This is that folder I told you about that had that nigga Malcolm's records inside it. But look who else's name is in it!"

Trigger looked over the papers Boss held out for him, and he read the name out loud that Boss pointed to: "Destiny Moore!"

"That's the same bitch I met at the gas station!" Boss told Trigger. "Read this right here!"

Trigger looked back at the papers and read aloud what Boss was pointing at: "Step-sister Destiny Moore! Step-mother Patricia Warren!"

"This bitch thinks she's slick, baby bruh!" Boss said with a smirk. "She knew who the fuck I was, and now she's trying to play the set-up game."

"So what we gonna do?" Trigger asked, hoping Boss was about to let him have some more fun.

"Relax, baby bruh!" Boss told Trigger, knowing what his boy wanted.

He pulled out his phone and pulled up Destiny's number and hit send to call her.

He then looked over at Trigger and said, "I've got a plan for shorty."

"Oh, now you decide to call me, Boss," Destiny answered the call after two rings with an attitude.

“My fault, shorty,” Boss told her in a soft voice that turned into a lowered voice. “Let me make it up to you. Can I see you tonight?”

Chapter 1

DESTINY HUNG UP THE phone with Boss after setting up a date to meet him later that night. She quickly got up from the bed and rushed into her bathroom to run some hot water in the Jacuzzi-style bathtub. She added some scented bath oil to the water, and while the tub filled, she walked back into the bedroom.

Destiny picked out a Dolce & Gabbana outfit she knew perfectly hugged her body. She laid the outfit across the bed and then picked out a black silk thong and bra set before heading back into the bathroom, only to hear her cell phone begin ringing. She shut off the water and rushed back out into the bedroom to snatch up her phone, and then answered without checking to see who was calling. "Who is this?"

"Why haven't you called me back, Destiny?"

She recognized the voice as her boyfriend's and continued undressing.

"Scott, I've been busy working. I told you before I left that it was going to be like this!"

"So why call me then? When I call back, you don't answer the phone or even answer my message I leave on your phone."

Destiny sighed as she lowered her body into the hot water. She shut her eyes as she laid her head back against the tub.

"Scott, I'm sorry, baby! I've just been dealing with this mess Malcolm has gotten into out here in Miami. I promise to try calling you more often though, Scott."

Destiny continued her phone call with her boyfriend, listening to him complain as usual. She sat and wondered exactly why she was still even with his ass, when she thought about his thick nine-inch dick he carried between his legs and the fact that he was next in line to take over his father's empire in Portland, Oregon.

Destiny ended the call with Scott after promising to call him the following day. She then laid down the phone on the floor outside the tub and instantly began thinking about the extremely handsome Mr. Boss.

~ ~ ~

"Boss, are you serious?" Vanity asked her man, after hearing the bullshit he had just told her.

"You're standing there asking me for permission to go out with some bitch who's the step-sister of Malcolm Warren and who's trying to set you up!"

"Vanity! Relax, babe!" Boss told her as he reached out

to her, only to have her snatch away from him. He then sighed loudly and deeply.

"Vanity, I know it's crazy what I'm asking, but you know where my heart is, and I thought you trusted me, ma!"

"I trust you. It's this bitch or any bitch around my man who I don't trust, Boss!" Vanity broke down to him.

She then folded her arms across her chest and stared hard into his eyes.

"Where exactly are you taking this bitch, Boss?"

"I'm not taking her anywhere, Vanity!" Boss admitted. "She's planning to take me somewhere."

"Where?"

"That I don't know."

"This is bullshit, Boss!" Vanity said, turning away from him.

She started toward the bathroom, only for Boss to grab her by the waist and wrap his arms around her. He then hugged her back up against his chest.

"Babe, don't overreact! Just trust me!" Boss told Vanity, speaking softly into her ear. "Vanity, you're my heart. Just trust me! You trust ya man, right?"

Vanity was unable to fight against her man, so she closed her eyes as he spoke into her ear. She listened to the smoothness of his voice. She then gave in and turned around in Boss's arms to face him. She wrapped her arms around his waist and laid her head against his chest.

"Boss, I trust you. I'm begging you not to hurt me. Do whatever you gotta do, but remember that you have your woman and family here waiting for you."

"I love you, shorty!" Boss told Vanity, kissing her lips as she squeezed him tighter.

Once Vanity was calm and inside the shower, Boss joined her; and just as he expected, they ended up making love. After driving Vanity to three orgasms, he finally exploded and released inside of her. After washing each other afterward and then climbing out of the shower, Boss began picking out something to wear while Vanity put on a pair of panties and one of his T-shirts. She then sat down on their bed and watched him as he dressed.

"How do I look?" Boss asked, once he was finished dressing in cream-colored Kenneth Cole slacks, a matching short-sleeve button-up, and a pair of Kenneth Cole suede loafers with a cream Kangol cap.

"You're not wearing a jacket?" Vanity asked, standing up from the bed and walking over to Boss's side of the closet.

She picked out a coffee-cream-colored leather jacket and

walked back over and helped him put it on.

"There you go. That finishes the outfit. I love you, Boss."

"Love you too, shorty!" Boss told Vanity as he picked up his keys, phone, money, and burner.

But before he left the bedroom, he grabbed Vanity and passionately kissed her.

"Call me if you need to or want to talk to me. I have nothing to hide, ma!" he said as he turned to leave.

Vanity smiled as she watched her man walk out of their bedroom. She then fell back onto her bed and sighed, just as her cell phone began to ring.

~ ~ ~

Destiny looked at her watch for the fourth time and noticed it was 7:25 p.m. She held off pulling out her cell phone and calling Boss's number, because she did not want to appear that she was anxious to see him. She instead got up from the couch, left the den, and headed toward the kitchen, only to hear her cell phone begin to ring back in the den. Destiny rushed out of the kitchen and headed back into the den. When she pulled her phone out from her purse, she saw that it was Malcolm on the other line. She answered her step-brother's call with a bit of an attitude.

"What do you want, Malcolm?"

"Why the hell ain't you call me back? What's going on with Boss?"

"Malcolm, you're sounding just like Scott when he called me earlier. I'm going to tell you the same thing I told him before. I'm trying to fix this mess you've made, and I'm waiting on Boss to call me now."

"Call you for what?"

"Malcolm, you just need to—. Hold on!" Destiny told her step-brother, hearing knocking at her front door.

She left the den and walked over to the front door. She looked out the peephole and saw it was Boss. With a smile on her face, Destiny told Malcolm she would call him back as she hung up before he could say anything. She took a deep breath and released it, trying to calm herself down. She then unlocked the door and opened it wide.

"You really love testing me, don't you, Boss?"

"You look good, sexy!" Boss told her, ignoring her comment.

He watched as her expression changed, even though she was trying to fight it.

"You wanna come in?" Destiny asked, rolling her eyes at Boss as she stepped back and allowed him inside.

She then turned around and looked him over while he

stood looking around her condo. She had to admit that not only was Boss a gorgeous man, but he was also probably the best-dressed guy she knew besides her step-father, Malcolm Sr.

"Would you like something to drink?"

"I'm good, gorgeous!" Boss replied as he turned to face Destiny.

He put on a show, looking her over while walking slowly around her and making a full circle.

"You're really gorgeous! I'm really loving the way the outfit is fitting you," Boss told her with a smile, once he stopped back in front of her.

"Thank you," Destiny replied, looking away from Boss as she began to blush. "Let me get my purse and we can leave."

Boss watched Destiny walk away and noticed the added twist in her walk. He shook his head and waited until she reappeared carrying a Dolce & Gabbana purse.

"You ready, gorgeous?" Boss asked with a smile.

"Yes, Boss!" she answered as she intentionally brushed up against him and caught the scent of his strong but smooth cologne. "You smell good."

"I was thinking the same thing about you," Boss told her

as he also intentionally brushed up against her as he stepped outside, catching the smile that spread across her face.

After locking the front door and turning to follow Boss out to his car, Destiny smiled when she recognized Boss's 2009 model Porsche Twin Turbo.

"Nice car!"

"Thanks!" Boss replied as he unlocked and then opened the passenger door for Destiny.

He caught her eye as she put on a show while climbing into his car.

Chapter 2

"IS IT AN ACCURATE guess to say that you're into exotic, fast cars?" Destiny asked Boss as she sat in the passenger seat of his Porsche Twin Turbo looking around as he sped away from her condo.

Boss shifted gears and then glanced over at Destiny, only to find her watching him. He focused back on the road.

"Yeah, pretty much!" he responded with a grin.

"So, if you don't mind me asking," Destiny began as she turned as much as she could in her seat to face him, "how exactly do you afford these types of cars? I remember when we first met you were driving a Ferrari, right?"

"Good memory!" Boss answered, before quickly asking, "So, where exactly are we going? You still haven't told me."

Destiny gave Boss the address to where the two of them were headed. She then changed the subject back to their original conversation.

"So, are you going to tell me what is it you do that allows you to buy these types of cars, Boss?"

"Investments," Boss answered, glancing over at Destiny again.

"Investments, huh?" Destiny repeated, giving him a

small smile while staring at him.

She then picked up on his refusal to explain any further by the way he answered with only one word. Destiny decided to let the subject drop for the time being.

"So tell me, Boss, you have a Porsche and a Ferrari, but do you have a Lamborghini too?"

"Not as of yet!"

"Why not?"

"Remember, I'm new down out here!"

"I almost forgot!" Destiny stated. "I tell you what. If things go right tonight, we can see a friend of a friend of mine who works at an exotic car dealership."

"If things go right tonight, huh?" Boss repeated with a smirk, cutting his eyes over to Destiny.

~~~

"Hey, girl!" Vanity said while opening the front door for Gigi.

After she stepped inside, Vanity shut the door and locked it behind her.

"Where are Boss and Trigger at?" Gigi asked as she and Vanity walked into the front room and sat down on the white leather sofa.

Gigi also set down the bags of Chinese food containers
~~~

that she had brought with her.

"Boss's ass is out with Malcolm's sister, and Trigger is in Miami dropping off stuff for Boss's people," Vanity explained while ignoring the surprised look her best friend was giving her.

"I know damn well you're gonna tell me exactly why Boss isn't handling his business or home with you instead of out with Malcolm Warren's sister?" Gigi stated. "And why the hell you even let his ass go out with some other bitch?"

Vanity explained everything Boss had told her, but she was unable to go too deep into detail since Boss had not yet explained every part of his plan to her. Vanity was just finishing up her conversation with Gigi when Boss's little friend walked into the room.

"Hey, Lloyd. You hungry?"

Lloyd shook his head.

"Where's Boss?" Lloyd asked.

"He had to deal with something. He'll be back later," Vanity explained. "Is there something wrong?"

Lloyd shook his head again.

"Would it be okay if I played with the PlayStation?"

"Sure. Go ahead, sweety!" Vanity told him with a smile as Lloyd walked over to the television.

After turning on the TV, he found a game and then turned on the game system.

"So, I guess you've got a new son, huh?" Gigi told Vanity, whispering over to her girl while watching the young boy who Boss had brought home to live with the two of them.

Vanity slowly smiled at the thought of actually having a family with Boss. She then excused herself from the front room and walked into the kitchen, only to return a few minutes later with a paper plate, a glass, and a can of soda. She then made up a plate of Chinese food for Lloyd and walked over to him. She set it down along with the glass and soda, to which she received a smile and a thank you.

"I guess that's my answer, momma!" Gigi playfully told Vanity, smiling once she returned back to her seat.

~~~

After they arrived at their destination, Boss found out that Destiny was taking him to a dinner and comedy theater. Boss parked the Porsche, and then both he and Destiny climbed from the car. He hit the locks by remote as Vanity boldly walked over to him, intertwined their fingers, and held his hand. The two of them entered the building a moment later and watched the hostess nod in greeting to
~~~

Destiny. It was obvious she recognized Destiny, which wasn't a surprise now that Boss knew who she was. Boss allowed Destiny to lead the way to a table at the front of the stage.

"I see you've got a lot of admirers already," Destiny stated once she and Boss were seated side by side at their table.

"I see you're pretty well known here," Boss stated while ignoring what Destiny had just said. "I thought you said you weren't from Miami either. How's it that the hostess recognized you?"

"I didn't lie, Boss," Destiny said, before she quickly added, "I have been in Miami a few times before, and I've been here a number of times as well."

"It was only a question, Destiny," Boss told her as a waitress walked up.

It was evident to Boss at how quickly Destiny tried to cover her slip-up. They both ordered something light to eat. Once the smiling waitress finally tore her eyes away from Boss and walked off, Destiny spoke up.

"Boss, can I be honest with you about something?"

"What's up, gorgeous?"

Destiny blushed at the nickname he had given her, and

then she slowly shook her head while holding his eyes.

"Boss, I'm really attracted to you, and I know you've said you have a woman, but I can't help wanting to be more than just some friend you call from time to time. I want to at least be able to go to sleep at night with you lying beside me, even if I know when I wake up the next morning you won't be there. I want to have you a part of my life in some type of way. I understand we just met, and I know this is fast, but I've never met anyone like you. You have this way about you that's very attractive, Boss."

Boss heard and recognized the game for what it was, so he simply nodded his head and remained silent. He then turned his attention back to the stage as the show began.

~ ~ ~

Destiny felt a certain way after expressing herself to Boss, only for him to completely ignore everything she had just said to him. She barely ate or drank anything and really didn't pay much attention to the comedian on stage.

"What's on your mind, gorgeous?" Boss asked, leaning over and speaking into Destiny's ear in a voice just above a whisper.

Destiny turned her head and looked over at Boss. She was a little surprised at the anger she felt after hearing his question.

"Boss, what type of question is that?"

"Are you going to answer the question?" Boss asked, glancing from the stage over to Destiny.

He could tell she was upset, probably because she was always used to getting her way.

"Boss, I can't believe you!" Destiny stated, folding her arms across her chest. "I just sat here and expressed to you what I felt and wanted with you, and you said nothing. What the hell do you think is on my mind, Boss?"

Boss calmly looked around the room and saw people at different tables staring at the two of them after Destiny had raised her voice at him. Boss then looked back at Destiny.

"I heard you loud and clear, Destiny. I need only to hear you to understand you. I'm a man of action, not of talking," he calmly responded.

"What the hell is that supposed to mean, Boss?" Destiny asked him.

She looked down at his hand once he laid his palm up on the table in front of her. She then looked back at Boss and met his eyes.

"You having second thoughts, gorgeous?" Boss asked with a smirk on his lips.

Destiny broke out into a smile when she realized exactly what Boss was telling her. She then took his hand and happily intertwined their fingers.

~ ~ ~

Destiny was deep in thought in the ladies' restroom supposedly using the toilet. She was barely listening as the line rang on her call to her step-father. The voice message picked up and requested the caller leave a message. Destiny left a quick message telling her father to call her back, and then she hung up. Destiny then thought a brief moment about calling her step-brother's number, but she decided against it.

Destiny left the restroom after washing her hands, and instantly spotted Boss waiting for her. He had some company from a blonde white woman, who was all up in his face flirting and smiling with him. Destiny instantly felt a strong sense of jealousy.

"Baby, you ready?" Destiny asked, walking right up on Boss and stepping between him and the blonde woman.

Boss slowly smirked after witnessing her show of jealousy.

"It was nice meeting you, Helen. I'll give you a call soon," Boss said as he looked back to the other woman.

"Excuse me?" Destiny cried with an attitude, placing

both hands on her hips. "You plan on doing what with her, Boss?"

"Let's go!" Boss told her as he started out the exit with an upset Destiny following behind him.

"Boss, let's get one thing—!"

"Relax, Destiny!" Boss told her, cutting her off in the middle of what she was saying.

He hit the locks to the Porsche by remote and walked up to the driver's side while ignoring the attitude Destiny was shooting at him.

Once the two of them got into the car and pulled out of the parking lot, Boss finally addressed her attitude.

"Understand something, Destiny. If you plan on dealing with me, then I'ma need you to grow up and act like a woman!"

"Whoa! Excuse me, Boss!"

"All this questioning me about every little thing I do isn't necessary," Boss continued, ignoring Destiny's interruption. "As a man, I'm going to either carry myself as a man or basically do what the hell I want. It's up to you to trust that I'ma hold shit down as a man, or just say fuck me and do you. What's it gonna be?"

"I just want to know!"

"The question was what was you going to do?" Boss reiterated, cutting off Destiny.

Destiny sucked her teeth and rolled her eyes at Boss in anger. But she was amazed at how sexually excited she was just from his take-charge attitude and arrogance. She folded her arms across her chest and stared out the window.

"I won't repeat the question, Destiny," Boss stated, with an edge to his voice that caused her to look over at him.

"I hear you, Boss. I'm not going to ask any more questions about what you do."

"You drink?" Boss asked with a smirk.

"A little! Why?"

"You'll see!"

Destiny sighed loudly after quickly realizing that was the only answer she was going to receive from Boss. So she just relaxed in her seat and reached over and laid her hand on his right thigh. She caught the look Boss gave her, but he remained quiet.

Destiny began to notice the area into which Boss was driving after they had finally begun having a conversation. She then looked over at Boss as he pulled up in front of a liquor store.

"Boss, what are we doing here?" she asked.

"Getting something to drink," Boss answered as Berry came rushing out from the liquor store to the car.

"Hey there, Boss man!" Berry greeted Boss, bending down into the driver's window.

"How's everything out here?" Boss asked, looking over to the team Rico had set up in front of the store.

"Everything's good!" Berry confirmed.

Boss nodded his head in approval and then pulled out a knot of cash, peeled off a few bills, and handed them over to Berry.

"Do me a favor. Go inside the store and grab me a fifth of Hennessy."

Boss watched as Berry took off to do what he was asked. Boss then looked over at Destiny.

"How exactly do you know him?" she asked.

"He's just a friend of mind," Boss replied, shifting his attention back over to the team that was working the new crowd buying the Blue Devils.

~~~

Vanity stared at the clock while lying in bed. She was really beginning to get upset and even thought about calling Boss, but she refused to even pick up the phone and call him. She told herself she trusted what he told her he was going to
~~~

be doing.

Vanity rolled over on her side just as her phone began ringing. She snatched up the phone beside the clock on top of the bedside table.

"Hello."

"You still up, ma?"

Vanity sighed and felt the weight lifting from her chest at the sound of Boss's voice. She relaxed, rolled over onto her back, and shut her eyes.

"Where are you?"

"On my way home! You miss me?"

"Boss, don't ask me that! You know I miss your behind!"

"Go ahead and ask."

"What?"

"Vanity!"

"Yes, babe!"

"Go ahead and asked the question on your mind."

Vanity slowly smiled at how well her man knew her.

"So, what happened tonight?" she asked with a soft sigh.

Vanity listened as Boss told her everything, from going to the comedy club with Destiny Moore to Destiny almost begging him to cheat with her on the side, even after he told her he had a woman.

"So what now, Boss?" Destiny asked once he finished his explanation.

"Vanity, don't worry! Whatever I decide to do, I'll let you know first. That's my word!" Boss admitted.

Vanity smiled at the promise her man had just made to her, which made her relax even more.

"Hurry up and get home. I want my man next to me!"

Chapter 3

BOSS WAS UP EARLY having breakfast with Vanity, Trigger, and Lloyd before he and Vanity took Lloyd to the new high school she had selected for him to attend. Boss stuck through the entire process of getting Lloyd enrolled into school. He then gave the boy $200 before he and Vanity left the school. Once Boss and Vanity were in the school's parking lot, Boss walked Vanity over to her car.

"Am I seeing you later?" she asked.

"Aren't you supposed to be meeting up later on to do the whole meeting with the builder and designers for the club?" Boss asked, causing Vanity to smile, since she was certain he had forgotten.

"I love you!" Vanity told him, still smiling as she kissed his lips. "I'll see you later, and don't forget you have to meet Willi Brown about that order you had me put in."

"I ain't forget, woman!" Boss stated, lightly slapping Vanity on the butt as she was climbing into her Stingray.

Boss waited and watched Vanity as she drove away from the parking lot. He then headed over to his Porsche and climbed inside after hitting his remote locks. He backed out of the parking space and pulled off, leaving the high school.

Once on the road, he dug out his phone and hit Trigger's number.

"What's up, big bruh?"

"Where you at?"

"I just got to the spot to meet up with Eazy and the others. What's up?"

"Let everybody know I'll be there soon. I gotta handle something real quick."

"You good?"

"Yeah! I'll hit you when I'm close by."

Boss hung up with Trigger, only to have his phone ring a moment later. He glanced down at the screen and answered.

"What's up, Destiny?"

"Hey, you! You busy?"

"Not fully. What's up though?"

"Can you meet me just for a few minutes? Please! I have something for you."

"What is it, Destiny? Can it wait?"

"Boss, it's just gonna take a few minutes. Can you just do this for me?"

"Where you at, Destiny?" Boss gave in while shaking his head.

~ ~ ~

Destiny had hung up with Boss over twenty minutes ago, and she was now checking her watch for the fourth time. She looked up, just as her business friend walked up beside her.

"He's still not here yet, Suzy!"

"Have you tried calling him? Oh my God!" Suzy called out, switching from what she was saying when she noticed an insanely gorgeous guy who just walked into the dealership. "Who is that?"

Destiny turned around to see who Suzy was talking about, only to break out in a huge smile when she saw Boss had finally arrived. She walked over to him and wrapped her arms around his neck.

"I thought you wasn't coming."

"I said I would," Boss replied. "What's up though? I don't have a lot of time."

"Come on!" Destiny told him, smiling as she took his hand in hers and then led him over to where Suzy remained standing in the middle of the dealership staring directly at Boss. "Suzy, this is my friend, Boss."

"Boss?" Suzy asked as she held out her hand to him.

"ReSean!" Boss corrected. "Everyone calls me Boss."

"Suzy Spagnollo," she introduced herself while shaking

hands. "So, you and Miss Moore are friends, huh?"

"Suzy, Boss doesn't have a lot of time. Can you show him the car, please?" Destiny cut in, not liking the look or tone the dealer was giving Boss.

Suzy motioned for Boss and Destiny to follow her as she led them across the dealership in front of a brand new model Lamborghini.

"Lamborghini Huracán LP 610-4 Spyder!" Boss stated, recognizing the car as he slowly walked around the drop-top crystal-blue car.

"You seem to know your cars, ReSean," Suzy stated, impressed with his knowledge.

"Do you like it, Boss?" Destiny asked him with a smile.

Boss nodded his head yes and then looked over at Suzy.

"How much is it?"

"Don't worry about it, Boss!" Destiny told him, pulling out her ringing phone.

She looked at the screen and saw it was step-brother calling.

"Suzy, go ahead and do the paperwork."

Destiny walked off from Suzy and Boss and answered the call.

"What is it, Malcolm? I'm busy!"

"What the hell is your problem?"

"First of all, who are you yelling at, and secondly, what are you even talking about anyway?"

"What the hell are you doing taking Boss to the fucking comedy show last night? Fuck do you think this is?"

"Malcolm, I'm going to ask you again. Who do you think you're yelling at, boy?" Destiny repeated, looking over at Boss and Suzy. "Last time I checked, Malcolm sent me out here to deal with this mess, and that's what I'm doing. I will say this one time only. If I find out you are having me followed, we will have a problem!"

Destiny hung up the phone and then turned her focus back toward Boss and Suzy, only to find them both gone.

~~~

After Boss found out from Suzy that Destiny was putting up the money for the Lamborghini, he changed plans by giving Suzy the money for the car as her commission. He then filled out the paperwork and paid for the Lamborghini himself. After that, Boss began discussing a business proposal with the female car dealer.

"So, if you could come across the money to open up your own dealership, would you?" Boss asked as an idea began forming inside his head.
~~~

"That's always been my dream!" Suzy confessed. "I know a few good locations, and I've gained a lot of business friends who would be willing to do business with me if I opened up a dealership of my own."

"What about if you had a business partner?" Boss asked her. "A silent business partner, that is!"

"Who exactly are you speaking of, ReSean?" Suzy asked, staring at him with a questioning expression on her face.

"Let's just say that since I have a love for exotic cars and you're licensed to do this type of work, I'm willing to put up half of what we need to open a dealership. What do you say?"

"Are you serious, ReSean? You got that type of money?"

"What do you say, Suzy?" Boss asked again, just as there was a knock at the office door.

Suzy looked up from staring at Boss to see her co-worker, Carl Brooks, and Destiny standing at her office door. Suzy then stood up from behind her desk and smiled.

"Thanks, Carl. I've got it."

"Why'd you two leave?" Destiny asked, looking from Suzy to Boss and then back to Suzy.

Boss stood to his feet and spoke directly to Suzy.

"You have my number, Suzy. Give me a call when you've made a decision."

"Boss, you're leaving?" Destiny asked, trying to stop him. "What about your car?"

"Suzy is taking care of everything for me," he told Destiny. "Call me later. I gotta go!"

Destiny watched as Boss simply walked out of the office without a backward glance. She wanted to yell in frustration; instead, she spun around to face Suzy.

"What happened with Boss?" Destiny demanded.

~ ~ ~

Boss left the Lamborghini dealership and drove across town to meet up with Eazy and the others. He saw that everybody was already at the apartment he was renting for Gina, since she only wanted something simple in the Miami Gardens neighborhood. Boss parked the Ferrari inside the complex next to Eazy's truck. He then locked the Ferrari, entered the complex, and walked up to Gina's apartment. When he knocked, he heard music coming from inside.

"Hi, ReSean!" Gina cried out happily after opening the front door and seeing him.

She hugged him and then allowed him to come inside.

"Is everything alright with the apartment?" Boss asked

as Gina locked the door behind them.

"Everything is great, ReSean! Thank you for everything!" Gina told him, kissing his cheek. "I'll leave you to your friends. Do you need anything before I go to the back?"

"I'm good, Gina. Thanks!" Boss told her, before she turned and started to the back of the one-bedroom apartment.

He then walked over into the living room, where Eazy and the team were waiting.

"What's up, big bruh?" Trigger spoke first, standing up and embracing Boss.

"What's good, team?" Boss asked, after releasing Trigger and looking around at the others.

Boss made eye contact with each person before he sat down beside Eazy across from Black Widow and Savage.

"I hope each of you understood what was said yesterday, and for those of you I called and spoke with, everything we've discussed begins today. I've already had Trigger go over to the west side of Miami, and I've already set up the areas where each of you are going to control and set up spots. As I said before, muthafuckas are either with us or they're with the morgue!"

Boss looked around at each face.

"I've already had the Blue Devils put together and divided for each crew. Trigger, you got that?"

"Sure do!" Trigger replied as he stood up from the couch and disappeared into the back of the apartment.

Boss continued the discussion with Eazy, Black Widow, Savage, Butter, Joker, Rico, and Magic, when Trigger re-entered the room carrying two extra-large duffel bags in each hand and a backpack around his shoulders. Boss sat back and watched as his boy set down all three bags in front of him.

"I've bought gifts, people!" Boss announced.

He then bent forward and first opened the two duffel bags and then the backpack, showing all three bags were filled with automatics and semi-automatic rifles.

"Happy holidays, people!"

Chapter 4

MALCOLM JR. SLAMMED DOWN his phone to keep from throwing it against the wall after just ending a phone call with his father, who spent the entire call yelling at him about the mayhem that was happening on the west side of Miami. Malcolm not only had to deal with his father's rants, but also calls from Curtis Black asking for help. As well, a few hustlers were calling questioning him about who Boss was and where he came from. Malcolm then called his step-sister and began pacing the floor, listing to the phone ring until Destiny finally picked up the line.

"What, Malcolm?"

"Let me guess! Malcolm called you too, didn't he?" Malcolm Jr. asked his sister as he sat down on the edge of his desk. "I just hung up with him as well."

"We need to do something about Boss, Malcolm! Malcolm's talking about coming to Miami, and I'm not trying to deal with his ass right now!"

"What happened to this so-called plan you've set up?"

"I can't make something happen when I can't even talk to him! Since this mess started over in Curtis Black's area, Boss hasn't been answering my calls, and I've heard his name over and over all over the city, Malcolm!"

"I already decided what I'm going to do, but I need you to get in contact with him. I need you to get him away from his team that he's always with, and I'm going to have his ass hit!"

"Well, let me work on getting his ass on the phone. I'll call you back."

After hanging up with Destiny, Malcolm pulled up another number and called it. He once again began pacing across the room until the person on the other end answered.

"Yeah!"

"It's Malcolm. I got a job for you!"

~~~

Destiny listened to the line ring while she called Boss again. She sucked her teeth once his voice message answered. She then hung up the phone even more upset because of the fact that Boss was blatantly ignoring her for the past three days, after they last saw each other at the Lamborghini dealership. Destiny sighed and started to call Boss's phone number again, when the phone rang inside her hand. When she looked down at the phone screen, she couldn't help the smile that spread across her lips.

"You finally decided to call me back, Boss."
~~~

"I've been busy!" Boss stated. "What's up though? You just called me."

"I need to see you, Boss."

"Why?"

"What do you mean why?" Destiny asked with an attitude. "I want to see my man! Is that a problem?"

"Pretty much!" Boss replied. "I don't see us doing us any further, shorty."

"What?" Destiny yelled. "What the hell do you mean, Boss?"

"I mean, this is our last conversation, but tell Malcolm I said he's next on my list after I'm done with Curtis Black!" Boss told her, before briefly pausing and continuing. "Since you're his step-sister, I figure you could get him the message faster than someone else!"

Destiny was shocked and completely surprised after what she just heard Boss tell her. She wasn't even aware he hung up the phone since she was so caught up in trying to figure out how he knew she was Malcolm's sister. She called Malcolm back and waited two rings when he answered the phone.

"Yeah, Destiny!"

"Malcolm, we got problems!"

"I already know that! What's new?"

"He knows!" Destiny told Malcolm. "Boss knows I'm your step-sister."

"What? How the fuck he know that?"

"I'm still trying to figure that out now! I don't have no idea, Malcolm!"

"Well, it don't matter anyway. I just put out a $25,000 hit on his ass! Fuck it!"

~ ~ ~

Boss hung up on Destiny after letting on that he knew who she was. He then slowed down his Porsche in front of Mom & Pop Diner, where he was supposedly meeting Curtis Black. He parked his car, just as Savage and Black Widow drove by in Savage's Dodge Ram 2500. Eazy then pulled up in his truck and parked beside them.

"Looks like ol' boy also bought backup," Trigger told Boss, staring inside the diner from the passenger seat of Boss's ride.

"I see 'em!" Boss replied as he smirked and climbed out from his Porsche, with Trigger following right behind.

Boss locked up his Porsche and started across the parking lot while Eazy and the others fell into step with him. Boss stepped into the diner first, after Savage opened the door and held it open for the others.

"We're finally meeting, Boss!" Curtis stated, seeing the young boy who walked up to the table at which he and four of his boys were sitting. Why don't you have a seat?"

Boss wasn't really feeling the clown in front of him and really wasn't in the mood for friendly conversation at the diner. But he went ahead and sat down across from Curtis, with Trigger on his right and Eazy on his left.

"Let's make this quick and easy, Black! I'm sure you received my message, so what's it gonna be? Are you getting down or not?"

"Whoa! Relax for me, youngin'!"

"Answer the question!" Boss told Curtis.

"Who do you think you're talking to?" one of Curtis's shooters spoke up while staring hard at Boss.

"I'm pretty sure it wasn't you!" Trigger spoke up, shifting his eyes over to the homeboy on Curtis Black's left.

"I'm pretty sure if you need some attention though, I'll be more than enough!" Savage added as he folded his massive arms across his wide and muscular chest.

"Whoa!" Curtis Black cried out, feeling the quickly building tension in the diner. "How about we all just calm down and talk like businessmen. This doesn't have to get out of control."

"Then how about answering the question?" Boss demanded in a calm and chill voice while locking eyes with Curtis.

Curtis slowly shook his head and said, "I'm sorry, man; I can't give in to your demands; but I can offer you a business deal that I'm sure you will agree with."

"No need!" Boss stated as he stood to his feet, turned, and started toward the exit, along with his team following behind him.

~ ~ ~

Curtis watched the young hustler as he and his team left the diner without responding to his attempt at a new offer to do business instead of giving him full control of the streets. Curtis Black then looked over at his right-hand man.

"What you think, Tone?"

"I think you should let me murder the muthafucker!" Tone answered nastily, still staring as Boss and his people left the diner's parking lot.

"I'm sure that would be a lot harder than just saying it!" Curtis said as he looked over at his team of shooters spread to his left and right.

Curtis nodded for his team to leave, since everything was

finished and Boss and his gang were gone.

"I really think that boy's gonna be a problem," Smoke stated, before he continued. "I agree with Tone, Curtis, man! If you won't let us get at the dude, then I think it's best to put money on that nigga's head!"

"I was actually thinking the same thing!" Curtis stated as he stood up from his seat.

He pulled out his phone as he and his two men were heading toward the exit. Curtis then pulled up a number from in his phonebook. Just as he stepped outside the diner and started toward his Range Rover, Tone grabbed his arm and stopped him, never giving him the chance to call the number he had pulled up.

"What the fuck is this nigga doing?" Tone asked, nodding over toward the Porsche that was parked across the street and sitting at the corner.

Curtis instantly recognized the same Porsche Boss had arrived and left in. He then looked down at his phone as soon as it began ringing inside his hand. The name and phone number were withheld; however, Curtis was certain he knew who was calling.

"Wrong decision!" Boss said.

Just when Curtis heard Boss's voice, he looked up when

he heard the scream of tires. Curtis stood in complete shock as a dark blue Jeep Grand Cherokee Sport appeared out in front of the diner and the back doors flew open.

~ ~ ~

Boss watched from behind the tinted windows of his Porsche with a laughing Trigger. Boss sat emotionless as he watched Curtis Black and his boys get chopped up by the hit team he had on standby just in case there was a need.

"Did you see them clowns' faces?" Trigger asked as Boss pulled off and left the scene.

"Yeah! I seen them!" Boss replied.

But Boss was already thinking ahead and putting together a plan in his mind how a change was going to be put into effect.

"So now that this nigga, Curtis Black, is no problem anymore, when are we getting at this clown-ass nigga, Malcolm?" Trigger asked, unknowingly cutting in on Boss's thoughts.

"I'ma send him the same message Black got!" Boss told Trigger. "But I want everyone to be ready; because from what I read inside that file, this nigga Malcolm's pop is a real old-school gangster and don't got a problem dropping niggas and adding to the body count!"

"How the fuck a nigga like that breed a pussy like that nigga Malcolm?" Trigger asked, sadly shaking his head.

"Don't slip, baby bruh!" Boss told Trigger as he began schooling his boy. "Don't let that act that nigga Malcolm's putting on fool you. Don't just anybody sit where he's sitting in the game and they ain't got no gangster in them, even if your pops gave you the crown. You still gotta put in major work to hold on to the empire. You feeling me?"

Trigger nodded his head in agreement after just listening and taking in the game that Boss just gave to him. Trigger sat in silence replaying the words his mentor had just said to him.

Chapter 5

VANITY NOTICED THE LOOK on Lloyd's face as soon as she pulled up in front of his school ten minutes late. She began feeling worse than she already did once she saw the look on her little man's face.

"Hey, man!" Vanity said, smiling as Lloyd climbed into her Stingray. "I'm sorry I'm late. I got caught up in all the business at the club. You mad at me?"

Lloyd shook his head no and then said, "It's okay. Tina just left a little before you came. I got to talk to her a little."

"Tina?" Vanity asked, smiling over at Lloyd. "Who's this Tina?"

"Just this girl in two of my periods," he replied. "Vanity, how do you know if a girl likes you or is just being nice to you?"

"Why do you ask?" Vanity said while smiling at Lloyd. "Do you think Tina likes you?"

"I've never had a girlfriend. And it's like every time Tina sees me, she's smiling and waving at me. Then after school she waited out front for you with me, but left after it got too late."

Vanity smiled even harder after hearing what her little

man had just told her.

"Man, do you trust me?"

"Yeah!"

"All right then. This is what I want you to do. The next time you talk to Tina ask her for her phone number and—"

"She already gave it to me!" Lloyd interrupted Vanity. "She wrote it down and gave it to me."

"We'll work on it together then," Vanity told him with a smile. "You forgive me for being late?"

"Sure, Vanity!" Lloyd replied, looking over at her with a grin.

Vanity heard her phone begin to ring as she and Lloyd were talking. She dug out her phone from her bag and saw that Boss was on the other line.

"Hey, babe!"

"What's up, ma? Where you at?"

"I just picked up Lloyd from school. Where are you?"

"Handling something. But why are you just picking up Lloyd? He's been out of school almost twenty-five minutes now!"

"Boss, I was busy at the club. I've been dealing with the builders and the people designing how I want everything. Then I had to deal with helping Gigi with the girls who were coming in to talk to us. I've been really busy, and before I knew it, it was time to pick up man!"

"Put 'im on the phone!"

Vanity sucked her teeth at Boss's attitude as she passed the phone over to Lloyd.

"Boss wants to talk to you, man."

Lloyd took the phone from Vanity and placed it to his ear.

"What's up, Boss?"

"What's up, lil' man? You good?"

"Yeah!"

"School was good?"

"Yeah! It was cool."

"A'ight. I'ma take you to go get a car, but you can't drive until you get your license. So tell Vanity I said you need your license and also you need a phone. I'ma see y'all in a little while. Tell Vanity I love her, lil' man!"

"Here, Vanity!" Lloyd told her, handing back the phone after Boss had hung up.

"Boss hung up?" she asked, seeing that the call had ended.

"He told me to tell you that I need to get my license and I need a phone. And Boss told me to tell you that he loves you too."

Vanity smiled at the message relayed to her from Lloyd. She shook her head and then turned toward Lloyd.

"What type of phone you want, man?"

~~~

"I can't believe this shit!" Malcolm yelled after just hearing the news about Curtis Black and his top lieutenants being gunned down after supposedly having a sit-down with Boss and his people.

"So what now?" Destiny asked, hearing the news while seated on the other side of Malcolm's desk. "I warned you that Boss wasn't your normal hustler, Malcolm! There's something very familiar about him and his arrogance!"

"Fuck that muthafucka!" Malcolm yelled, snatching up his phone just as it began ringing inside his fist.

Malcolm saw that the name and number were withheld, and he almost ended the call from coming through but instead answered. "Who the fuck is this?"

"Is that how you answer the phone, Malcolm?"

Malcolm instantly recognized the voice on the other end of his phone. He felt his heart speed up as his anger shot sky-high.

"Muthafucka! You really got the nerve to call me!"
~~~

"This won't take long!" Boss told him, ignoring his outburst. "I'm offering you the same offer Curtis Black was offered. You can either do business with me and only me, or you can shut down everything! Think about it!"

"You mutha—!" Malcolm began, only to hear the cell phone end in his ear.

He had to catch himself before throwing the cell phone across the room.

"Malcolm, what happened? Who was that?" Destiny asked, seeing the rage on her step-brother's face.

"That was your little boyfriend!" Malcolm got out through tight lips. "This muthafucka thinks he's ready to play this game. I'm about to show him how to play!"

Destiny watched Malcolm make a phone call on his phone a few minutes later. She heard him speak to someone named Perry and then someone named Peter. Destiny then witnessed with her own ears as her step-brother put out an even bigger hit on Boss than the already $25,000 he had on his head.

~~~

Boss made a few stops and checked on some spots. He wanted to show his face and check up on Berry, whom he left with a cell phone that he bought for him along with $200.
~~~

Boss then drove over to the restaurant at which he was a silent partner with Eazy's parents and ordered five dinners to go. He then spent a few minutes with Momma, Evelyn Collins.

After leaving the restaurant and driving over to Gigi's apartment, since she wasn't working, Boss chilled with Trigger at her place a few minutes and gave Gigi one of the dinners. Boss promised her he would stop by her apartment early Saturday to make the trip out to Indian Town so she could see her husband.

Boss drove away from Gigi's apartment a little while later and headed north. He stopped at a gas station and slid up to an open pump. He shut off the car, and then both he and Trigger got out.

"How much?" Trigger asked as he started toward the gas station entrance.

"Twenty!" Boss answered. "And grab me a bag of strawberry Starburst candy."

~~~

"Here we go now!" Prince whispered over to his right-hand man, Murder Mike, after trailing Boss all across town and finally catching him slipping. "Let's do this shit!"

Prince and Murder Mike grabbed their hammers and then
~~~

climbed from the Buick Regal. They crept across the parking lot and came up on Boss's blind side. Prince moved too fast when he swung up his burner and fired.

Boom! Boom! Boom!

Boss ducked at the first sound of a gun going off, just seconds before his driver's side window blew out. He ignored the sting he felt across his neck as he snatched his Ruger from his waist.

~ ~ ~

Trigger reacted instantly after hearing the gunshots. He dropped the bag of Starburst candy and took off out of the store, pulling out both his Glock 17s as he burst through the door.

Boom! Boom! Boom! Boom!

Trigger saw Boss behind his driver's door letting off rounds through the busted window. Trigger wasted no time letting both his bangers speak.

Brrrrrr! Brrrrrr! Brrrrrr!

Trigger rushed out in the middle of the gas station toward the two clowns who were ready to die. He caught one of them and dropped his ass as the other one took off running.

~ ~ ~

Boss saw Trigger take off running behind the other hit

man. Boss walked over to the man who Trigger had dropped and looked down on him, only to see that it was Murder Mike.

"Fuck you, mutha!"

Boom! Boom!

Boss cut off Murder Mike with two shots to the face. He then rushed back to his Porsche and jumped inside. He quickly sped out of the gas station parking lot and drove in the direction in which he saw Trigger take off.

~ ~ ~

Trigger walked up on the fallen gunman as he lay beside a parked Chevy Impala, bleeding from the bullet holes in his chest. Blood rushed from his mouth. Trigger raised his banger and let his Glock speak.

Brrrrrr!

Trigger heard the engine and looked over just as Boss pulled up in his Porsche. Trigger then glanced back to the body before hopping into the car.

"Who the fuck was that?" Trigger asked as Boss flew out of the neighborhood they were in.

"Remember that nigga Victor I told you about?" Boss asked Trigger. "That was two of his boys I got at when I first got to Miami."

"Well now they're with their homeboy!" Trigger stated. "But I think we need to get you checked out, big bruh."

"Checked out for what?"

"You're bleeding bad! Your neck!"

Boss reached up and felt the wetness. He looked at his hand and saw blood. Boss instantly felt his anger rise, because he got caught slipping and could be dead right now if not for Trigger.

Chapter 6

AFTER THE ATTEMPT ON his life, Boss turned up on the streets, adding to the body count he already had growing and giving Detective Aaron Wright more work to do. He also let Malcolm know he no longer had a decision to make in starting a war with Miami's supposed kingpin.

Boss dealt with the quickly building war with Malcolm while dealing with Vanity at home, who suddenly was becoming very overly protective of him after the attempt on his life and the wound he had received to his neck, which was actually just a cut from where the bullet grazed his skin. A few days after the war started, Boss again caught himself in the middle of an attempt. This time he was with Trigger and Black Widow walking out of a Burger King with breakfast.

Boss was careless about putting on a show while dealing with the two hit men he barely saw coming, but he caught the flare from the chrome one of the men was pulling from his waist. He saw the gun and first got out his Ruger; and before either Black Widow or Trigger knew what was happening, Boss was letting off shots while walking in the two men's direction, dropping one and then the other. Boss stood over both men, and without questioning them to find out who sent them, because he really did not care, he emptied the magazine into both of their bodies.

"Yo, Boss! Let's go!"

Boss looked back at both Trigger and Black Widow, who were now sitting inside the Ferrari. Boss glanced back at both bodies before jogging over to the car and hopping into the driver's seat.

"How'd you know?" Black Widow asked from the backseat as Boss peeled away from the parking lot.

"I just caught the movement!" Boss replied, taking out his phone and pulling up Detective Wright's number, before tossing the phone over to Trigger.

"Let the detective know what's going on and where to find the bodies."

"Boss, you think that was a hit from Malcolm?" Black Widow yelled over the wind.

"I know it was him!" Boss yelled back. "And that's why we returned the hit!"

~ ~ ~

"Yeah!" Malcolm said, answering his phone while riding inside his G-Wagon with Moses behind the wheel.

"Malcolm, it's Destiny. Where are you?"

"About to handle some business. Why?"

"I'm sure you'll hear about it, but your hit team, Perry and Peter, missed."

"What the fuck you mean they missed? They never miss."

"Well, they missed Boss!" Destiny stated. "Right now as we speak, there's a huge crowd outside the parking lot of a Burger King off of 22nd and 41st."

"Damn it!" Malcolm yelled out, before taking a deep breath. "Let me call you back, Destiny!"

After hanging up with his sister, Malcolm hated what he was about to do, but he pulled up a number from his cell phone and made a call.

"Detective Shaw."

"It's Malcolm, Shaw! I need a favor."

"Well I'll be damned! If it ain't the great Malcolm Warren Jr.! What a surprise, considering all the shit that's been happening in your part of the city since some young hustler took over Curtis Black's section. What exactly can I do for you?"

"Not over the phone! Meet me at my place in two hours."

"This isn't a friendly visit."

"You'll be taken care of."

"I'll be there."

After hanging up the phone with the detective, Malcolm looked over at Moses.

"So, it's this serious, huh?" Moses asked.

"I just plan on ending this bullshit with this muthafucka sooner rather than later!" Malcolm told his bodyguard and best friend while already thinking up a new plan to get rid of Boss.

~ ~ ~

"Lloyd!"

Lloyd heard his name as he exited the school and entered the student parking lot. He looked behind him to see Tina breaking off from her friends and rushing over to catch up with him. He turned to face her as she jogged to a stop in front of him.

"What's up, Tina?"

"Hey, Lloyd. I just wanted to know if you wanted to come to a party tomorrow with me? It's a friend's birthday."

"Sure! I'll go with you."

"Okay! I'll call you tonight and we'll talk about it. I need to get going."

Lloyd accepted the kiss to his cheek Tina gave him. He smiled as he watched her walk off and head back to her friends. Lloyd turned and started walking toward his new 2009 model Mercedes-Benz SL65 Black Series. He hit the remote and unlocked the door, and then he opened the back door and tossed in his backpack. He climbed behind the wheel and started up the Benz. He then backed up out of the parking space and started toward the parking lot exit.

After pulling out of the lot and making a right turn, Lloyd instantly spotted a crowd, but he locked in on Tina arguing with a dark-skinned guy. Lloyd pulled up and hit the brakes. He was out of the car before he realized it and was rushing around the front of the Benz and straight up on the dude who was yelling in Tina's face.

"You got a problem, nigga?" Lloyd yelled, shoving homeboy back out of Tina's face.

He then gently pushed Tina back a bit.

"Who the fuck is you?" homeboy asked as he walked back up into Lloyd's face.

"I'm her boyfriend," Lloyd got out. "Whatever problem you got, you and me can deal with it."

"Boyfriend?" homeboy asked with a smirk on his face.

The homeboy looked off as if looking at the others around him, but then he tried sneaking Lloyd.

Lloyd saw through the guy's bullshit before he actually

swung. Lloyd was already ducking when he smashed a right to the guy's stomach, knocking the breath out of him. While he was bent down at the waist and holding his stomach while trying to catch his breath, Lloyd swung a left that connected to the side of the guy's face, knocking him down and out. Lloyd stared down at the dude, but he was aware of the whispers coming from the crowd around him. He looked from the sleeping guy on the ground toward Tina.

"You alright?"

Tina nodded her head, and a small smile appeared on her lips. She said nothing as Lloyd took her backpack.

"Come on! I'm taking you home," he informed.

Lloyd walked back over to his Benz and tossed Tina's backpack inside alongside his in the backseat. He then opened the passenger door for her to get in, shut it behind her, and then walked back around to the driver's side and got inside the car.

After pulling off and leaving the crowd staring at them, Lloyd looked over at Tina and saw her staring at him and smiling.

"What?"

"Were you serious when you told Tod you were my boyfriend?"

"I was just . . . I mean . . . ummmm!"

"Do you want to be my boyfriend, Lloyd?"

"Do you want me to be?"

"Yes!" Tina answered, smiling even more.

She reached over and took Lloyd's right hand into hers while he steered with his left, and began admitting the truth.

"I've been wanting to talk to you, Lloyd. The boy you just beat up is my ex-boyfriend. I broke up with him because I was going to ask you to be my boyfriend tomorrow at the party."

"Do you have to get right home right now?" Lloyd said, smiling at what he was hearing.

"Why?"

"Because I want you to meet someone."

"Okay," Tina replied with a smile. "Let's go!"

~ ~ ~

Vanity was tired but busier than she was the day before, since the club's grand opening was scheduled for the following night. She picked up her ringing cell phone just as she was finishing the paperwork in front of her.

"Hello!"

"What's up, ma? You busy?"

Vanity smiled at the sound of her man's voice. She set

down her purse and then leaned back in her tall black leather office desk chair.

"Hey, babe! What's up?"

"Missing you. Can you get away from the club for a few minutes? I'm at the house alone and need you here too."

"Oh really!" Vanity stated, but then caught on to something Boss said. "Boss, where's Lloyd? He's supposed to be home from school already."

"Relax, ma! Lil' man's probably at the boxing gym that me and Trigger got him signed up at."

"Boxing gym?"

"Yeah! He's been going for maybe three months now."

"And why am I—? Hold on!" Vanity told Boss, after hearing the knocking at her office door. "Come in!"

"Vanity, you busy?" Gigi asked, sticking her head inside.

"I'm just talking to Boss. What's up?" Vanity asked.

"You've got visitors," Gigi stated, opening up the office door wider and allowing the guests to walk inside.

"Oh my God!" Vanity happily cried as Lloyd walked into her office.

Vanity got out of her seat, walked over to him, and gave him a hug.

"Man, what are you doing here? I thought you were at

the gym."

"Ummm! I brought somebody to meet you," Lloyd told Vanity, nodding to the left of her.

Vanity looked to her left and was surprised to see the young girl standing there. She was even more surprised at how unbelievably beautiful she was.

"Lloyd, is this Tina you told me about?"

"Hello, Lloyd's mother!" Tina said, holding out her hand to Vanity.

Vanity shook the young woman's hand and then remembered Boss was on the phone.

"Man, Boss is on the phone!"

Lloyd left Vanity and Tina to talk. He then walked over to Vanity's desk and picked up the phone, only to see that Boss was still waiting.

"What's up, Boss?"

"Lil' man?"

"Yeah, what's up?"

"What's up, lil' man? Fuck is you doing out there?"

"I brought my girlfriend out to meet Vanity," Lloyd explained. "They're talking right now!"

"Girlfriend, huh?"

"I was going to tell you."

"Relax, youngin'!" Boss told Lloyd. "Handle your business, lil' man."

"Ummm! Is it cool if I go to a party with Tina tomorrow?"

"It's cool with me, but holla at Vanity and make sure she's cool with her. Tell her I said to call me later and that I love her."

"I got you," Lloyd replied, smiling before hanging up the phone.

Chapter 7

BOSS WAITED OUTSIDE IN front of the townhouse with Trigger, Eazy, Rico, Butter, and Joker, with a blunt in his hand and two more on rotation while Vanity and the other women finished up inside. Boss handed the blunt he was smoking off to his right to Trigger.

"So, lil' man Lloyd's at some party with his lady, huh?" Eazy asked.

"Yeah!" Boss proudly smiled at the mention of his lil' man. You should see his lil' shorty though, E. Baby girl's cute as hell!"

"Who's cute as hell?" Vanity asked as she was walking out of the front door with Gigi and the other women behind her.

"We talking about my lil' man's lady," Boss admitted while looking over Vanity in her Dolce & Gabbana pantsuit that was perfectly showing her curves.

"Calm down, big boy!" Vanity told Boss, seeing the look she instantly recognized on his face whenever he wanted her. "We've got business to handle, but momma will take care of you tonight."

Boss smiled as he stood watching Vanity walk out to his

Lamborghini Spyder that he bought a few months back and was going to drive for the first time. He pulled out his keys and hit the remote to unlock the doors.

"Let me get that, beautiful!"

Vanity smiled as she looked back and saw Boss walking up behind her in his Tom Ford suit with a thigh-length black leather jacket. Vanity allowed her man to open the door to his Lambo for her.

"Thank you."

"Thank you!" Boss stated, watching the way her slacks hugged her perfectly rounded phat ass.

"We're going to be late, Boss!" Vanity told him, smiling while catching where his eyes were directed.

Boss shook his head and smiled. He then shut the car door, walked around to the driver's side, and saw that everybody was waiting on them.

Once they were inside the car, Boss started it up and backed out of the parking spot in front of the garage of the townhouse. He pulled off and enjoyed the smooth yet powerful sound of the Lambo's engine.

~ ~ ~

"My God!" Vanity cried twenty minutes later, once Boss turned the Lambo onto the street where the club was located.

She couldn't believe the line of cars, SUVs, and trucks going up and down the road, all trying to gain entrance through the security gate. "Babe, do you see this?"

"I see it!" Boss stated while steering the Lamborghini on the outside of the line of cars until he reached the front gate entrance.

"Mr. Holmes, Mrs. Holmes!" a security guard stated after recognizing both Boss and Vanity.

He then nodded his head, released the front gate, and allowed them to pass.

"Boss! Babe, do you see this crowd?" Vanity said in complete disbelief as the valet took care of the Lambo.

They stood waiting until Trigger, Eazy, and the others joined them. They then entered the club as a group. Boss smiled proudly as soon as he entered the club with Vanity and the others. He dropped his arm around her waist and spoke into her ear.

"This is what's up, ma! I'm loving it, and good work!"

Vanity kissed Boss's lips just as a hostess appeared. The young woman then escorted them to the VIP section in front of the stage. Vanity stood smiling as the pretty half-naked girl walked her man and their friends through the club.

~~~
~~~

Lloyd arrived at the house party which Tina had told him about, and she led him into the front yard of the two-story house. Lloyd noticed a few familiar faces from school and received a few nods of greeting, just as he and Tina were surrounded by a crowd of girls and a few guys.

"Tina, you gotta get Lloyd outta here!" Shanna told her best friend as she pulled Tina and Lloyd back toward the front gate.

Tina pulled away and demanded to know what was going on.

"Tina, it's Javon and—!"

"There goes lover boy!" Tina heard as Shanna was trying to talk, only to look up to see both her ex-boyfriend, Javon, and his brother.

She grabbed Lloyd's arm just as Javon rushed Lloyd.

"Watch out!" Lloyd yelled, snatching away from Tina as Javon wrapped up with him.

He smashed two blows to Javon's ribs, which caused him to yell out in pain.

~ ~ ~

Boss just barely heard his phone ring over the loud Rick Ross song playing throughout the club. He then dug out his phone and saw that Black Widow was calling him.

"What's good, Black?"

"Boss, we got bad news!"

"What happened?" he asked, sitting up in his seat.

He listened as Black Widow explained about the hit attempt on Malcolm that turned into an all-out shoot-out, with Malcolm and his bodyguard getting away.

Boss slowly smirked at the news he had received. "Let the nigga breathe for now. Get to the club!"

Boss hung up with Black Widow, just as Vanity, Gina, and six dancers entered the VIP section. Each of them was carrying a bottle of champagne inside a steel ice bucket. Boss smiled as Vanity walked straight over to him and stepped in between his legs. She sat back against his chest onto his lap as a thick honey-brown-skinned, exotic-looking woman began to dance in front of them.

"What do you think?" Vanity asked Boss as the two of them sat back and watched the girl sexily move her body for them.

"You talking about the girl or how the club turned out?" Boss asked while still watching the girl.

"Both!" Vanity replied as she began grinding and riding the print inside of Boss's slacks.

Boss felt his phone vibrate inside his pocket and dug out

his phone to answer it.

"Mr. Holmes!"

"Who's this?" Boss asked, not recognizing the voice.

Boss glanced at the screen to see Lloyd's name and number.

"Mr. Holmes, this is Tina. Lloyd told me to call you and tell you what happened."

Boss listened to his lil' man's girlfriend tell him about the fight Lloyd had been in that led him to being in jail. Boss lifted up Vanity from his lap and then motioned over to Trigger and the other guys to follow him.

"Boss, where you going?" Vanity yelled over the music to him.

"To pick up my lil' man!" Boss replied as he walked over to the elevator but instead headed quickly to the stairwell around the corner.

~ ~ ~

Lloyd was unsure how long he was actually waiting inside the holding cell after first being fingerprinted. He was allowed to make one phone call. Tina told him she had called his father, who was on his way. Lloyd thought back to the fight and felt his left eye that was almost completely swollen shut.

"Lloyd Marshall!"

Lloyd heard his name right before the cell door was opened. He stood to his feet, only to have the guard announce he was bonded out. Lloyd walked behind the guard along with Javon and his brother, or best friend, whoever the guy was who helped Javon. They all followed the guard after he slammed the cell door shut, and they then made their way toward the front of the jail. Lloyd was released fifteen minutes later after being printed a second time, signing some paperwork, and picking up his property.

"Lloyd!"

Lloyd recognized the voice as soon as he stepped outside, and then he saw Tina rush toward him. He made it down the ramp just as she threw herself into his arms and hugged him tightly.

"Oh, baby!" Tina cried, seeing Lloyd's eye. "Are you okay?"

"I'm good!" Lloyd answered as he looked to his left and saw Boss, Eazy, Trigger, and most of Boss's team.

He then stared at Boss and tried to see if he was pissed off at him.

"Come on!" Tina said, taking Lloyd's hand in hers and then leading him over to where Boss stood.

"Boss, I can explain, man."

"Relax, lil' man!" Boss interrupted him. "Yo' lady already told me how you held her down twice against the same dude. You alright though?"

Lloyd nodded his head yes as Tina walked up beside him. She wrapped her arms around his waist and lay in against him. Lloyd looked down at her and then back at Boss, only to receive a wink from him.

"Here!" Boss said, tossing the keys to the Lambo to Lloyd. "It's still early. Go take your lady out and finish your date, lil' man."

Lloyd accepted the money Boss gave him as well as an embrace. Lloyd dropped his arm around Tina's arm and let her lead him out to Boss's car. Once they were inside the Lamborghini, Lloyd noticed the way Tina was smiling at him. He started up the engine and pulled off.

"I really like your father, Lloyd. Mr. Holmes reminds me of my father," Tina began.

"You mentioned him before," Lloyd stated. "He wasn't home when I came to pick you up. He work at night or something?"

"He works out of state, so he doesn't live with me and my mother. They're not even together."

"Where does he live?"

"Chicago. He's into the street like your father, but he's a lot older than Mr. Holmes and he's from Miami."

"Miami?" Lloyd asked, looking from the road over at Tina. "What's your father's name?"

"Malcolm!" Tina answered. "Malcolm Warren."

~ ~ ~

Boss made it back to the club some time later after having Trigger take him by the house to pick up his Ferrari. Boss led the team back into the club and headed to the VIP area. Black Widow and Savage were already there, along with another female who looked like Black Widow but with a scar that ran down over her left eye and stopped mid-cheek. It was still sexy looking to Boss, however.

"Who's the girl?" Boss asked as he walked over to the booth and sat down. "And where's Vanity and the others at?"

"Boss, meet my twin sister, Princess," Black Widow introduced. "Vanity and the others just left to look around, and your lady took the men to another VIP area they had set up for them."

"You wanna explain why you got your sister here and what happened with that nigga Malcolm?" Boss questioned her while motioning to Eazy to roll up a blunt.

"To answer your question," Princess stated, drawing everyone's attention toward Boss, "the muthafucka is supposed to be dead; but it seems this Malcolm actually has men who are willing to die for him, since I was aiming directly at the fool's head."

"Black!" Boss called to Black Widow while holding Princess's eye.

"Yeah, Boss?" Black Widow answered.

"Is Princess with us or what?" Boss asked.

"I'm standing right here, so if you have a question, you can address it directly to me!" Princess said.

Princess heard chuckling coming from her right side, and looked back to the young boy who was laughing.

"Do you find something funny with what was just said, little boy?"

"I'ma let the whole little boy comment go this time, but it's clear you don't know who you're dealing with; and the only reason you're not added to the body count is because you is Black Widow's sister," Trigger replied with a smile.

"And who exactly are you, little boy?" Princess asked as she turned to face Trigger.

"Baby bruh!" Boss spoke up, since he already knew how Trigger was and that he had no problem dropping a female just as fast as he would drop dudes.

He then directed his attention back toward Princess. "Princess, I'll say this once. This team here respects each other, and how you're popping off at the mouth, I believe in letting problems be handled in house. So if you're looking to work with the team, then I trust Black Widow's judgment. But if you got other plans, then you know where the exit is since you passed it when you walked in. You decide!"

Princess held Boss's eyes a few moments, and then she slowly began smiling a devilish-like smirk. She then called to her sister.

"I guess you was right, baby sister. This one is to my liking, and he's not bad looking either," Princess admitted.

"And he's also taken!" Vanity stated as she and the other women entered the VIP area, drawing everyone's attention.

She walked directly over to Boss and bent down to kiss his lips.

"How's man?" Vanity asked after a minute.

"He's cool!" Boss answered. "I sent him and his lady out to the movies or someplace to finish out their night."

Vanity nodded her head in satisfaction and then sat down on Boss's lap.

"So what's the problem now? Because I know

something's up by the way everyone is looking!" Vanity asked.

Chapter 8

BOSS HEARD THE RINGING from either his or Vanity's phone after only just getting home and inside the bed after the club had closed down for the night. He felt Vanity begin moving and soon nudging him to answer the phone. Boss opened his eyes and first looked to his right at the bedside clock and saw that it was almost 6:00 a.m. and that it was his phone that was ringing. He grabbed his phone and saw that Eazy was calling.

"Yeah!"

"Bruh, we got problems!" Eazy told Boss as soon as his voice came over the line.

Boss listened to Eazy explain about the problem they were having, and he soon found himself out of bed and putting on some metallic-black Polo jeans and stepping into a pair of tan Tims.

"Babe, what's wrong?" Vanity asked as soon as Boss hung up the phone.

"Two spots just got burned down and at least ten of the soldiers got picked up, some straight outta their beds!" Boss told her while putting on a blazer-style brown leather jacket. "I'ma see you in a little while."

"Call me!" Vanity called out as Boss grabbed his gun, keys, and money before snatching up his black and white Yankees cap.

Boss left his bedroom and started toward Trigger's room, just as Trigger was rushing around the corner putting on a black T-shirt. Boss simply told him to drive as the two of them started for the front door. Once they were outside and saw the Lambo parked in the driveway beside Trigger's truck, they both got inside the Chevy 1500. Trigger spoke up a few minutes after driving away from the townhouse.

"You think it's that nigga Malcolm who's behind this shit?"

"I'm guessing he probably is!" Boss answered while staring out his window.

Boss then let his mind wander about everything Eazy had told him over the phone.

~~~

Once they were in Miami, they met up with Eazy and the other lieutenants, and then got the full story on what was going on. Boss then contacted Detective Wright, who already knew the situation, since word was going around at the station that Detective Howard Shaw and a team of officers were supposedly behind all the arrests that were
~~~

made. Boss and Detective Wright continued discussing what had taken place, realizing that only his soldiers were the ones who were arrested.

After hanging up with the detective and asking Wright to find out everything he could on Detective Shaw, Boss then pulled up the bondsman's number that he used when he needed to bond out Lloyd. After speaking with him and explaining the situation to him, Boss told the bondsman to contact him for the money once his men were released from jail.

"What now, pretty boy?" Princess asked Boss once he was off the phone.

Boss remained quiet a few moments, and then began giving out orders to see what could be found out on the street. He then had Trigger ride with him while they looked around at the spots that were burned down.

"I'm coming with you two," Princess announced as she started behind Boss and Trigger.

Boss, Trigger, and Princess broke off from the others and made the rounds around the city to check on the different spots that had been set on fire. Boss was certain of his own assumption of what had taken place at his trap spots. His phone rang, and Boss saw it was Wright calling him.

"Yeah! What's up, Detective?"

Boss listened as the detective filled him in on all the information he had gathered about Shaw. Boss told Wright he simply needed Detective Shaw's address as well as the addresses of any of his other family members.

"What's the word, big bruh?" Trigger asked as soon as Boss hung up the phone with his paid detective.

"It's about time I erased this nigga Malcolm!" Boss stated. "This Detective Howard Shaw has got to go first though!"

~ ~ ~

Detective Shaw was smoking a Winston cigarette as he drove from the station and thinking about the work he put in while heading for home. He smiled thinking about the $6,000 that Malcolm Warren Jr. was handing over to him for the job he did on the boys who worked for Boss.

After pulling into the front yard of his house, Shaw turned his Lexus into the driveway and parked beside his wife's Cadillac SRX. The detective climbed from the Lexus a moment later and heard a voice behind him while he was locking up the car.

"Good morning, Detective!"

Detective Shaw spun around while reaching for his

sidearm, only to pause at the sight of the barrel of a chrome gun that was pointed directly at his face by a woman with a scar down the left side of her face. Shaw slowly raised his hands up into the air.

"A'ight. How about telling me who you are and what you want, lady!"

"Shut the fuck up!" was all he heard.

Someone stepped out of the darkness, walked up to the detective and removed his sidearm, and then patted him down and found his backup weapon on his ankle.

"Let's go!" Trigger said, pushing the detective across the front yard toward the front door, with Princess following alongside him.

Princess opened the front door and stepped inside, and saw that Boss was seated on the couch in the living room while the detective's wife and a white man stood only in their underwear a few feet to the side of him.

"Pretty boy, you've got visitors!" Princess announced.

Boss turned his head just as a brown-skinned guy and Trigger stepped inside his house.

"Detective Howard Shaw?"

Shaw stared at the familiar-looking young man seated on his couch. Shaw didn't know how he knew him, but he was sure when he asked him a question: "You're the one they call Boss, aren't you?"

"You've heard of me, I see!" Boss stated. "It's good of your wife and her friend to let us inside the house to wait for you. Have a seat, Detective."

Detective Shaw first looked over at his wife, who instantly looked away. He then froze when he recognized the man next to her as his partner who was supposed to be home sick.

"You muthafucka!" the detective yelled as he started toward his partner, only to feel cold steel touch the side of his face.

"Muthafucka! Act stupid and I promise you'll have the shortest lived acting career ever!" Trigger told the detective, only for Boss to speak up.

"Hold up, baby bruh. I think I'm understanding what's going on in here!"

"What's up, big bruh?" Trigger asked while still pressing his Glock to the side of the detective's head.

"Detective, how about telling us who this is with your wife," Boss said with a smirk on his face.

"This son of a bitch is supposed to be my partner!" Detective Shaw angrily spit out while staring hatefully at both his wife and partner.

"Hold on!" Princess said with a laugh. "You mean while this clown's out working for Malcolm, his partner was here fucking his wife and got caught in the middle of having his dick deep up in her?"

"That's why they ain't hear us come in. The bitch was screaming so loud!" Trigger stated, with a smirk on his face.

"The dick must have been good!" Princess stated as she looked over at the wife. "Was the dick good, girl? You can tell me!"

Boss saw the detective's wife look at her husband and then lower her eyes.

"Look at it like this, Detective. You have two choices. You can tell me everything you know about Malcolm and I won't kill you, or I'll kill you and still find out what I want to know. What's your decision?"

Boss was not surprised when the detective began running his mouth and telling him everything he knew while still staring hatefully at both his wife and his partner. Boss then slowly stood to his feet once the detective finished what he had to say.

"Well, Detective. I try to be a man of my word, so I won't kill you!" Boss informed Detective Shaw.

"I never said shit that I wouldn't kill your ass though!" Trigger announced, seeing the detective's body stiffen up.

Boom!

Princess smiled at the sight of the whole side of the detective's head being blown off. She then looked over at the wife, who was staring in shock at what had just taken place. Princess then gave her the same thing as her husband.

Boom! Boom! Boom!

"Nasty bitch!" Princess spit out at the now dead wife as she looked over at her partner.

But before she could move, another cannon went off.

Boom! Boom!

"Damn, nigga!" Princess whined after Trigger blew open the partner's chest. "You gotta kill every damn body?"

"I just beat you to it!" Trigger stated as he turned and started for the front door. "Let's go now!"

"You make me sick, nigga!" Princess said as she followed Trigger out of the house.

Once Trigger and Princess finally made it out to the truck, Boss was already on his phone making a few calls to get his soldiers ready to deal with Malcolm once and for all. However, Boss, Princess, and Trigger didn't notice the dark-colored Maserati Ghibli that was parked across the street from the detective's house that was actually sent to keep watch over Detective Howard Shaw.

~~~

Malcolm received the call that Detective Shaw, his wife, and partner were all dead, so he turned on the news to see the report himself. Malcolm sat thinking for a moment wondering what the detective had said to Boss. He quickly began calling people while walking out of his den toward his bedroom. Malcolm then called Destiny twenty minutes later while Moses was driving him away from his mini-mansion.

"What do you want, Malcolm?"

"Destiny, get out of the condo!"

"What?"

"I'll explain later. Just get the fuck outta the condo, and meet me at the Best Western in Fort Lauderdale."

"Fort Lauderdale?"

"Destiny, just do what the fuck I say!" he yelled, before hanging up the phone with his step-sister.
~~~

Chapter 9

MALCOLM HEARD ABOUT THE hits Boss was making around the city, and he was more certain than ever that Detective Shaw ran his mouth off, since four of his spots and his major warehouse in north Miami had been taken over. Malcolm had been ignoring his father's phone calls while trying to come up with a sure plan to get rid of Boss for good.

Malcolm stood out on the balcony of his penthouse when his phone rang. He saw that it was his step-sister, Destiny, calling, so he answered.

"What's up, Destiny?"

"So, you've been ignoring my calls, huh?" Malcolm Sr. said once his son answered the phone. "You not only left the city to this petty hustler who's got you terrified, but you've left my city in his hands. What in the hell is wrong with you, boy?"

"Dad, I've got this under control," Malcolm told his father, really not trying to hear his father yell in his ear.

"Boy, if you had this shit under control, the fucking mayor wouldn't be calling me about this young boy!" Malcolm Sr. yelled into the phone. "I'll be in Miami in two days. You will be receiving a call within an hour or less time.

Answer the phone!"

Malcolm heard the line go dead after his father finished talking. He shook his head sadly and felt tired of all the bullshit, just as his phone began ringing again. He did what he was told and answered the phone.

"Yeah!"

"Malcolm, it's Destiny."

"What do you want?"

"Malcolm, look! He called me through Momma's phone and forced me to call you on a three-way line."

"I repeat. What do you want?"

"I've got an idea, Malcolm," Destiny said with a sigh.

"Oh, really?"

"You remember that girl named Brandi? I think her dancer's name was Pleasure."

"I know who you're talking about, but what about her though?"

"I just recently ran into her and she's back from Miami, but she's staying with some other guy. She and I spoke. She heard about what's been going on here, and she's interested in helping us."

"How?"

"She's willing to testify about everything she knows

about Boss and even admit to witnessing Boss kill Detective Shaw."

"So basically she's willing to lie then?"

"Who knows other than me, you, and her, Malcolm?"

Malcolm looked at his phone screen and heard someone calling in. He told Destiny he would call her back later. He then hung up with his step-sister and answered the other line. "Yeah!"

"Is this Malcolm Warren Jr.?" the caller asked.

"That's whose phone you called!" he replied with attitude.

"Mr. Warren, sir. Please hold for Mayor Wiesel."

~ ~ ~

Boss allowed Vanity to talk him into buying a penthouse on Miami Beach and then go shopping. He let her handle all the shopping besides picking out what went inside the den and the game room. Both he and Lloyd took care of picking out things for those two rooms in the penthouse.

Vanity finally called it quits after six hours and seven stores later, and they left the store they were in to get something to eat. She sat in the passenger seat of the new Land Rover Range Rover Sentinel that Boss spent a lot of money on, since the SUV was fire-, grenade-, and bulletproof.

"Baby, I've been thinking," Vanity stated.

"I know what that means!" Boss said, getting Lloyd to chuckle from the backseat and Vanity to punch him in the arm.

"I'm serious, boy!" Vanity told him, sucking her teeth.

"A'ight, ma!" Boss said with a light laugh.

Vanity rolled her eyes and sucked her teeth again.

"I spoke with an old friend of mine who used to dance at Pink Palace when I was still there. She was telling me that they're talking about selling the place."

"So let me guess. You're thinking about going after it, right?" Boss asked, cutting his eyes over to her.

"Can I?" Vanity asked, leaning over and taking Boss's hand into hers and kissing the back of it. "It's just adding on to what we're already making from everything we already have now."

"That reminds me!" Boss started as he took his hand back and pulled out his phone. "I need to call Suzy about the new shipment on those Porsche Carreras and the Ferrari Spyders that I asked about for the dealership."

"So you're just gonna ignore my question, ReSean Holmes?" Vanity asked, calling him by his full name.

"You're going to do it anyway, so go ahead, ma!" Boss told her, just as Suzy picked up the phone.

Vanity smiled after she got Boss's approval, even though she actually was going to look into the club. It was in a good area, and she remembered how business used to be until the dancers all began leaving the club. Vanity dug out her phone and called the number she received from her friend.

They arrived at the Olive Garden in Aventura at which Vanity wanted to eat. Boss smiled at Lloyd and saw his lil' man on his phone talking with his lady. Boss then dropped his arm around Vanity's shoulder, when he heard his name called out.

"ReSean!"

Boss looked to his left in the direction he heard his name, only to pause when he recognized the person who called him. Boss felt Vanity pull away and step in front of him.

"What the fuck are you doing here, Brandi?"

"Ummm, I believe I was talking to ReSean!" Brandi said nastily, stopping a few feet in front of Vanity.

"Ma, relax!" Boss told Vanity, wrapping his arm around her waist before Vanity rushed Brandi.

Boss then spoke up to Brandi and said, "Give me one reason why I shouldn't do to you what you tried to help

Malcolm do to me?"

"ReSean. Baby, I'm—!"

"Bitch, don't get hurt out here!" Vanity spoke up, cutting off Brandi. "Boss, ain't your baby. Watch your mouth, ho!"

Brandi looked over Vanity with a look of pure hatred. Brandi simply rolled her eyes at Vanity and looked over at Boss.

"Baby, when you're ready to talk, I'm sure you can find me, since I hear you're the king of Miami now! Maybe I can help you get rid of Malcolm once and for all! Think about it!" Brandi suggested.

Boss stared at Brandi as she walked off toward an F-Type Jaguar. He then allowed Vanity to grab his hand and lead him through the parking lot and up to the front entrance of the Olive Garden.

~~~

Brandi watched as Boss entered the restaurant behind Vanity and some young boy. She then dug out her cell phone from her Chanel bag and pulled up the number she was given to call just in case she needed to.

"Hello!"

"This is Brandi. I got news about Boss!"

"I'm listening."
~~~

"As we speak, he's at the Olive Garden at the Aventura Mall with that bitch of his!"

"Are you sure?"

"I just spoke with him only a few minutes ago."

"All right. Let me call Malcolm, and I'll call you back."

Brandi smiled as she hung up the phone with Malcolm's step-sister. She then looked to her left just as her supposed boyfriend climbed into the Jaguar.

"You ready to go?" he asked as he started up the car.

~ ~ ~

"Boss!" Vanity called out, raising her voice after calling him twice before and not receiving a response.

"Yeah, ma?" Boss answered, losing his train of thought when he looked over and saw Vanity's upset face.

"You didn't hear me talking to you?" Vanity asked, all upset.

"Naw! My fault, shorty. What's up though?"

"Never mind!" Vanity said, rolling her eyes and looking away.

Boss shook his head and looked over across the table at Lloyd and noticed his facial expression.

"Lil' man, what's up? You good over there?"

Now Lloyd lost his train of thought when he looked up

to meet Boss's eyes. He held Boss's gaze a moment, when Vanity spoke up.

"Man, what's wrong?"

Lloyd was still holding Boss's stare before he finally spoke up.

"That woman said the name Malcolm. I even heard you guys also say the name, and the only Malcolm I know is the one who ran Miami for a while until Boss moved here. But I've gotta tell you guys something."

"What's up, lil' man?" Boss asked, sitting forward in his seat.

"I'm not sure, but I think the Malcolm you've been going through it with has a sister," Lloyd admitted.

"We know, man!" Vanity stated. "He has a step-sister."

Lloyd shook his head. "I mean a younger sister that's got his blood," Lloyd continued.

"What you saying, Lloyd?" Boss asked.

Lloyd stared at Boss for a moment and then finally spoke up again, telling him what Tina had told him about her father and who he was.

"Oh my God! Lloyd, why are you just telling us this now?" Vanity asked, looking over at Boss and seeing him already on his phone.

Vanity looked back at Lloyd and saw the way he was staring at Boss.

"It's okay, lil' man. Boss isn't mad with you."

"Let's go now!" Boss ordered as he stood up and then nudged Vanity and Lloyd out of their seats.

Vanity had learned a long time ago not to question Boss. So she got up and snatched up her bag as she and Lloyd followed Boss through the restaurant and headed toward the front entrance. Boss hung up the phone just as he led Vanity and Lloyd out the door of the Olive Garden. Just as Boss got to the edge of the walkway, he saw a Yukon SUV swing into the parking lot.

"Shit! Come on!" he yelled as he pulled out his Ruger from the front of his Gucci jeans.

Boom! Boom! Boom! Boom!

Boss let his Ruger speak as soon as the back door to the Yukon quickly swung open and out jumped the first gunman, who immediately fell onto his face after catching two slugs to the chest. Boss yelled for Vanity and Lloyd to keep running while continuing to let off rounds from his Ruger until it clicked empty. Boss then took off running and made it to the Land Rover just as a slug slammed into the upper right side of his back, slamming him against the front of the

SUV.

"ReSean!" Vanity screamed, seeing Boss hit and blood pouring from his back.

"Get in the car!" Boss screamed through the pain, making it around to the driver's side of the SUV and opening the door.

He made it inside the Land Rover and fell forward across the steering wheel in pain from the bullet he took in the back.

"Babe, are you okay?" Vanity asked, jumping from the bullets that slammed into the armored windows.

"Yeah!" Boss grunted as he sat back on his good side and handed over the Ruger to Vanity. "There's another magazine in the compartment on the door. Just hit the seat controller. Push down on it."

Boss got the SUV started and then hit the gas and flew from the parking space. He steered the Land Rover directly at the five-team hit squad and watched as they all dove out of the way. He yanked a left at the end of the parking lane. Once he made it out and onto to the main road, he checked his mirror and was not surprised to see the Yukon behind them.

"Call Trigger! Find out where the fuck everybody's at!" Boss yelled to Lloyd.

~ ~ ~

Trigger felt his phone vibrate in his right pants pocket, but he was unable to answer it while doing over 120 mph on his Suzuki GSX-R1000R. He had left behind Eazy and the others after receiving Boss's call for help with Vanity and Lloyd. Trigger gave the bike more gas and picked up even more speed as he flew through the streets and shot past all the other cars, SUVs, and trucks.

Trigger made it to Aventura and headed in the direction of the mall, when he spotted the Land Rover Boss had bought for Vanity. Trigger also peeped the Yukon that was following closely behind them. He held down harder on the gas throttle, causing the bike to hit its maximum speed.

~ ~ ~

"What the hell!" Vanity yelled, swinging her head around after seeing the blur of something shoot past them. "Was that Trigger just now?"

"Yeah!" Boss answered, peeping Trigger when he turned down the street heading the wrong way.

Boss looked at his rear-view mirror and saw Trigger now behind the Yukon and catching up fast.

"Oh my God!" Vanity cried as she sat watching Trigger ride right up to the driver's side and let off a burst of rounds from his Glock into the driver's window, making the SUV instantly lose control.

"What is he doing?"

Boss looked back through his rear-view mirror just in time to see Trigger stop his bike in the middle of the street. He then hopped off, only to pull out his second Glock and calmly walk over toward the Yukon and let off rounds from both of his Glock 17s. Boss smiled once the Yukon exploded a few moments later after taking so many rounds to the gas tank.

Chapter 10

SAVAGE MADE IT TO Gina's apartment with Eazy and the others all following. They had all left the area which Trigger made look like a war zone. Savage then helped Boss out of the car and into the apartment after he lost so much blood and was feeling really weak. Vanity called a friend she knew who was a nurse, and then she had Eazy get Boss out of his jacket and shirt.

Once Boss was naked from the waist up and then laid down on his chest, Gina went to work on him like a pro. Everyone else stood back watching the entire thing. By the time the nurse finally showed up, Gina had the bullet slug out of Boss's back and cleaned up. He was now asleep on the sofa.

"You did a really good job on him!" Nurse Ebony Jones told Gina, smiling at how good she did. "Was you ever a nurse?"

"No!" Gina admitted with a smile. "But I've had a lot of practice with my husband before he got locked up."

"Well, you should really think about going to school to become a nurse or even a doctor," the nurse told Gina.

Suddenly banging started at the apartment door, which

drew everyone's attention and caused the team to all pull out their bangers.

"It's Trigger!" Lloyd announced. "I called him and told him where we was."

"Smart thinking, youngin'!" Eazy told him while walking over and opening the door.

"Where's my brother?" Trigger asked as he rushed into the apartment.

"He's asleep and fine, Trigger," Vanity told Trigger while sitting on the arm of the sofa near Boss's head and rubbing his wavy, short hair.

Trigger saw the patch over Boss's back and saw his brother asleep, and he realized that he almost lost his only family when he was supposed to be there with him to watch his back. Trigger sat down beside the sofa and leaned his head over near his brother.

"I'm sorry, big bruh. I swear it'll never happen again," Trigger whispered.

~ ~ ~

"Son of a bitch!" Malcolm yelled, slinging his phone across the room after just finding out that another attempted hit on Boss had failed and the muthafucka got away again.

"Let me guess!" Destiny said while watching Malcolm

now pace the floor after his phone call. "Boss is still alive, huh?"

"This muthafucka really is getting on my nerves!" Malcolm growled while still pacing back and forth. "Who the fuck is this bitch nigga? Why won't he just fucking die?"

"You know we still have that other option I mentioned to you," Destiny reminded him, receiving a look from her step-brother that would have more than likely put fear in someone else's heart.

"I want this muthafucka dead, not in jail!" Malcolm shouted at his step-sister while trying to put together a new plan inside his head.

"So what are you going to do once Malcolm gets here?" Destiny asked him.

"What am I gonna do, huh?" Malcolm screamed, shooting Destiny an evil look. "I see I'm solo on this shit all of a sudden, since you was supposedly sent here to help me with all this shit!"

"I've given you a suggestion."

"And I told you that I want his ass dead, not safe and locked up in some jail! Come up with another fucking idea!"

Malcolm shook his head and began pacing again, but he paused after a moment and looked back at Destiny.

"Vanity!"

"Who?" Destiny asked him.

"The bitch you couldn't get Boss to leave!" Malcolm reminded his step-sister, only to receive an evil look from her in return. "The same chick who Brandi told you was with Boss at the Olive Garden when she called you."

"What about her?" Destiny asked with an attitude after Malcolm's statement.

"It seems that's Boss's lady, and from what you told me about how loyal he was to her that he wouldn't even mess around with you, I'm willing to bet that if we get to her, we'll get his ass!"

"And how exactly do you plan on getting to her if you don't even know where to find her at, Malcolm?" Destiny asked him. "I'm sure Boss has her ducked off somewhere or most likely guarded."

Malcolm considered what Destiny had just said and was sure she was probably right. He began pacing again but started his plotting and tried to come up with another plan to kill his nemesis, Boss.

~~~

Boss opened up his eyes and stared a few minutes until he realized he was staring at a picture of him, Vanity, and
~~~

Lloyd on the wall above the new dresser Vanity had purchased at Bed, Bath, & Beyond. When Boss started to move, he suddenly froze up from the sting that shot through his upper back, reminding him of the wound he had received. He waited a few more minutes before he began rolling over onto his good side. He then slowly raised up into a sitting position and realized he was in the master bedroom in the penthouse Vanity had talked him into buying.

Boss climbed from the bed and noticed he was wearing only a pair of gray Nike sweatpants and ankle socks. He took his time and started walking toward the bedroom door and then the staircase. He could hear Keith Sweat's "How Deep Is Your Love" playing from downstairs.

"Vanity! Pretty boy's up!" Princess called out when she saw Boss making his way down the stairs as she was exiting the kitchen.

"What?" Vanity cried out as she walked out of the kitchen behind Princess, only to instantly spot Boss coming down the stairs.

She called out to Eazy, Trigger, and the others outside on the rooftop terrace as she rushed toward Boss when he reached the bottom of the stairs.

"Babe, what are you doing out of bed?"

"What's up? What's going on?" Eazy asked as first he, then Trigger, and then the rest of the team all rushed back inside.

"Big bruh!" Trigger said, smiling as he rushed over to help Vanity with Boss.

He wrapped his arm around Boss's lower back and led him into the den.

Boss sat down on the cream-brown leather La-Z-Boy chair and sighed.

"Somebody give me something to smoke!"

"At least we know there ain't nothing wrong with his lungs!" Black Widow said, laughing along with the others.

"How do you feel, babe?" Vanity asked, standing beside Boss and putting her hands through his hair.

"I'm good, ma," Boss answered as he took the lit blunt Trigger handed to him. "How long have we been here?"

"A few hours," Vanity answered. "You remember what happened?"

"Yeah!" Boss answered, thinking about the attempted hit on his, Vanity's, and Lloyd's lives. "Where's Lloyd at?"

"He and his lady are in the home theater," Vanity responded, but continued after seeing the surprised look on Boss's face. "Lloyd felt we should leave Tina here so you could talk to her when you woke up. She's spending the weekend with us."

Boss nodded his head in acceptance and then met and looked into his best friend's eyes.

"You came through for us, baby bruh! I saw you handle business out there. Thanks for holding us down, family!"

Vanity smiled while watching Trigger embrace Boss and whisper something into his ear. Boss nodded in agreement.

"Babe, are you hungry?" Vanity asked after the two brothers had parted.

"Yeah!" Boss answered. "When did all the stuff get here?"

"Most of it came a while ago, but the rest should be here tomorrow morning," Vanity told Boss before leaving the den and heading into the kitchen.

Boss watched Vanity as she walked out of the den, before he then turned to Princess to talk to her. "I don't trust Vanity alone in the streets anymore whether it's here or back home, but mostly out here in Miami. From now on, and whether she agrees or not, I want you with her whenever she leaves this building. We good on that?"

"I'll play bodyguard to your woman, pretty boy," Princess told Boss, even though she was slightly jealous since she was really beginning to catch feelings for him.

"Black!" Boss said, looking to Black Widow. "I don't care what it's gonna take, but I want you to get that bitch Brandi. This is her second time she's tried to have me killed!"

"You want me to handle her after I find her?" Black Widow asked with an evil smile on her face.

"Naw!" Boss replied as Vanity entered the den again carrying a plate with a phat sandwich with three types of meats on it.

He thanked his woman and then looked back toward Black Widow.

"When you find her, bring the bitch to me. I'll deal with her!"

"Who?" Vanity asked Boss.

"Pretty boy wants to kill this ho Brandi!" Princess told her.

"Eazy!" Boss called out, looking to his boy. "It's about that time for us to make that trip out to Atlanta for the pickup from my boy Murphy."

"Whenever you're ready, we're ready, my nigga!" Eazy stated while nodding his head at Boss.

"Most of all," Boss began, looking around at his team

minus Joker and Butter, who he knew were out on the west side of town handling business, "I want this bitch-ass muthafucka Malcolm dead!"

~~~

Lloyd noticed a light coming from the doorway of the home theater room. He looked over Tina's head and saw Boss and Vanity breaking out in a smile. Lloyd stood up from beside his girlfriend and rushed over to Boss. He then threw his arms around his waist and hugged him tightly. Boss smiled as he returned the embrace and then rubbed his lil' man's back as Lloyd released him and then stepped back.

"You good, lil' man?"

"I was just about to ask you that!" Lloyd told Boss, looking him over. "You good?"

"Yeah! I'm good!" Boss stated, smiling at Lloyd and then looking over to where Tina was sitting. "Let's go over and talk to your lady, lil' man."

Boss walked over to the wide couches that were positioned in front of the screen. He slowly sat down beside Tina while Lloyd sat down on the opposite side of her. Vanity then sat down on the arm of the couch beside Boss.

"How you doing, Tina?"

"Hi, Mr. Holmes!" Tina said softly. "Are you okay?
~~~

Lloyd told me what had happened to you."

"I'm good," Boss replied. "Did Lloyd also tell you that I wanted to talk to you?"

Tina nodded her head. "He explained everything to me about my father and about me possibly having a brother who you're having a problem with."

Boss nodded his head in approval at Lloyd, but then focused back to Tina.

"What exactly is your father's name, Tina?"

"It's Malcolm Warren," Tina replied. "And, yes, he's from Miami, but he now lives somewhere in Chicago."

"Can you call him for me?" Boss asked her.

Tina nodded her head once again, and she then dug out her phone to call her father at the number he gave her to reach him directly.

~ ~ ~

Malcolm Sr. felt the spare cell phone begin vibrating inside the inner pocket of his suit jacket. He excused himself from his wife and their guests and walked toward the bathroom, with his personal bodyguard a few steps behind him.

He dug out his cell phone that was for his daughter only and answered the phone.

"Hello, sweetheart."

"Hi, Daddy! Are you busy?"

"Not for you! Are you okay?"

"Yes! But my boyfriend's father wants to talk to you."

"Boyfriend?" Malcolm Sr. repeated, surprised at what he just heard from his seventeen-year-old daughter. "We'll finish this talk after I'm done with this boyfriend's father, Tina!"

"I love you."

"Love you too. Put this guy on," he told his daughter, smiling while shaking his head.

"Malcolm Warren Sr.?" Boss inquired.

"Malcolm, what the fuck are you doing with my fucking daughter, boy?" Malcolm asked, hearing the familiar-sounding voice.

"Relax! This isn't your son, Mr. Warren."

"What? Who is this?"

"I'm sure your son, Malcolm, has mentioned me often."

"Boss!" Malcolm Sr. growled after realizing who was on the line. "If you lay one hand on my daughter, you son of a bitch, I swear to God I will tear that city up until I find you and murder you myself."

"Are you finished yet?" Boss calmly asked the Miami

legend. "My interest isn't in hurting my son's girlfriend. I'm only interested in you and me having a sit-down to talk business and see if we can come to some type of agreement."

"What do you have I could possibly want, boy?"

"Miami!"

Malcolm Sr. heard the arrogance in the young man's voice, and for some odd reason, he felt some type of respect with the way the young man was handling himself.

"When and where, boy?" Malcolm Sr. replied.

Chapter 11

MALCOLM SR. WAS NOT surprised to see the team of security that accompanied the young man, even after he allowed him to set up the location at which they would have their meeting. Malcolm Sr. sat watching as the four metallic Range Rovers and a metallic black Denali Yukon trailed behind a pearl-black Land Rover Range Rover.

Once the SUVs parked in the open lot in the middle of a field in Naples, Malcolm Sr. watched as the doors on the four Range Rovers and the Yukon opened and men with different types of submachine guns climbed out. The door opened to one of the Land Rovers, and a young-looking boy climbed out seconds before another guy only a little older stepped out from behind the wheel.

"So, is this the person who's been causing me all this trouble?" Malcolm Sr. said, once the back door of the Land Rover opened and a young man dressed in slacks and a Gucci short-sleeve, button-up shirt was visible.

"Sir!" Malcolm Sr.'s personal bodyguard, Ike, spoke up. "No disrespect, but I almost thought that was young Malcolm who got outta that SUV just now."

Malcolm Sr. thought the same thing, but chose not to

speak about it. He announced that he was ready to get out of the car. He waited for Ike to step out and get the security into position. Once his door was finally opened, he climbed out of his Mercedes-Benz limousine. He walked from the back door of the limo and started around to the front with Ike at his side. Malcolm Sr. met the young man known as Boss between the limo and the SUV, along with the young boy from the passenger seat of the SUV.

"Malcolm Warren Sr.," Boss spoke first, staring at the slightly familiar-looking older man, but not because he was the father of Malcolm Warren Jr.

"So, you're the young man who has my city in a crazed state!" Malcolm Sr. asked. "What is it you want to discuss, young man?"

"I'll make this simple for you since I'm sure you have other business to deal with. I'm willing to go into business with you out of respect for the work you put in that's made you one of Miami's most major legends. But understand that I've put in my own work in that city, and I've done what your son wasn't able to do, which is take over the whole city. No side hustles from muthafuckas not working with me or for me! Are we on the same page, Mr. Warren?"

"I'm listening, boy!" Malcolm Sr. told Boss.

"I'm sure you know as well as I do that war stops business from further progression. So here's what I'm willing to offer you. I will continue to sell my product, but I will also allow your people to work the product you have, and there will be no problems from my people. There can be a 65-35 split in the city. I'm sure that's agreeable, since I'm sure you have Chicago and both Flint, Michigan, and Hollywood, California."

"I'm impressed," Malcolm Sr. stated, once Boss finished speaking. "You've done your homework, but what would give you the idea that I would give over the city to you, boy? Why wouldn't I just kill you and all your men right now?"

Boss saw Malcolm Sr. raise his hand, yet he didn't bother looking around as more vehicles appeared and surrounded him and his men. Boss simply began to chuckle while staring Miami's legend directly into his eyes.

"You find death funny, boy?" Malcolm Sr. asked, staring hard at Boss.

"Tell me something, Mr. Warren. Who do you know that has lived from a sniper round to the heart or even to the forehead?" Boss said, still chuckling.

"Holy shit!" Ike yelled, looking at his boss.

Malcolm lowered his head and looked down at his chest,

only to see the motioning red beam that stayed in the area of his heart. He began to suddenly laugh as he looked back at Boss.

"You know, boy, I actually think I like you and your style. The whole sniper thing is a real nice touch. You came prepared!"

"I figured you would, too!" Boss told him. "My mother always told me when dealing in life to move like you're playing a chess game that you don't want to lose. Make calculated moves in everything you do."

"Who told you that?" Malcolm Sr. asked Boss, staring at him with an odd look.

"It's something my mother used to always tell me when I was young," Boss admitted.

Malcolm Sr. continued to stare at the young boy standing in front of him.

"You're not from Miami, are you, boy?" he asked.

"We're getting kind of personal, aren't we?" Boss asked, smirking at Malcolm Sr. "So what do you say about my offer?"

Malcolm Sr. nodded his head slowly while continuing to stare at Boss.

"Let me get back to you in a few days with an answer.

But leave me your number on my phone."

Boss watched as Malcolm Sr. turned and walked back to his limo, which caused his security team to all pack it up as well. Boss stood watching the old-school gangster until he disappeared inside the limo.

~ ~ ~

Malcolm Sr. pulled out his cell phone as soon as he and Ike were back inside the limo. He pulled up a number that he hadn't had to use in more than twenty-some years, only to find the number was no longer in service. He hung up the phone, thought a few moments, and then made a phone call to another old friend.

"Chief Cook!"

"So you're a chief now, huh, Jonathan?" Malcolm Sr. asked, with a smirk on his face.

Chief Jonathan Cook remained quiet a brief moment before speaking up. "Is this who I think this is?"

"All depends on who you think it is."

"Warren, is this you, man?"

"Long time, Jonathan."

"I'll be damned! It has been a long time. What's got you calling up ol' me?"

"I need information, Jonathan."

"Why am I not surprised? Who's it gonna be this time? And just so you know, you're all out of favors, so this is going to cost you."

"When has anything ever been free with you, Jonathan?" Malcolm. Sr. stated. "I need whatever information you can get me on a Brenda Holmes. Do you need her last known number?"

"No, I'll get it," Chief Cook told him. "Now let's talk payment."

"I'll have $40,000 for you once you've found me the information, Jonathan," Malcolm Sr. told the chief before hanging up the phone.

"Everything alright, boss?" Ike questioned after Malcom hung up the phone.

"I'm about to find that out now, Ike. Just as soon as I find out where this woman is," Malcolm Sr. replied while staring out of his window. "We're going to Atlanta, Ike. I want to check up on a few things myself."

Chapter 12

MALCOLM SR. HAD BEEN staying at a hotel in Atlanta for the past two days after his meeting with Boss. He finally received the call from Chief Jonathan Cook that he had been waiting for, which provided him with two phone numbers and a north Atlanta address. He decided to just stop by the address instead of calling. As Malcolm Sr. and Ike drove in a rental Mercedes-Benz S550 Executive, Malcolm stared out the back window. He not only thought about the one woman he actually fell in love with before his wife, but also that she no longer wanted him after he had a son with another woman, who was now his wife. With thoughts flowing through his mind, he now wondered if it could really be true.

Once the Mercedes began slowing and taking him from his thoughts, Malcolm Sr. turned his attention to the house at which his chauffeur was stopping. Malcolm Sr. climbed from the back of the Mercedes once Ike had opened the door for him. He then motioned for his bodyguard to remain with the car as he started around the back end, stepped to the sidewalk and through the gate, and then up to the front door. He knocked instead of using the doorbell, and then waited a brief moment. He began knocking again, but no one answered.

Malcolm turned around, faced the street, and then looked up the block and then in the other direction. He finally dug out his cell phone and was pulling up a number, when Ike called out to him. He looked up and over to his bodyguard, only to see a red Nissan Maxima pull up in front of the house and into the driveway.

"May I help you?" Brenda asked, after climbing from her car and noticing a man standing on her porch.

Malcolm Sr. instantly recognized her, realizing she was just as gorgeous as when he first laid eyes on her all those years ago. He stepped down from the porch and started walking toward Brenda. Brenda froze when she looked up from grabbing her grocery bags from the backseat. She then dropped a bag once her eyes locked on the man in front of her.

Malcolm caught the bag Brenda had dropped.

"It's good to see you still remember me, Brenda," Malcolm said with a small smile.

"Oh my God! Malcolm!" Brenda cried in disbelief, even while staring straight at him. "How did you find me? What are you doing here, Malcolm?"

"Can we go inside and talk?" he asked her while

motioning Ike over. "I think we really need to talk."

"Malcolm, it's been—!"

"I know!" Malcolm spoke up, cutting Brenda off while handing Ike the grocery bag he was holding. "It's been over twenty years. About the same age as our son."

Brenda was completely shocked and surprised at what she just heard Malcolm say to her. She quickly grabbed her purse from the car and then locked up her Maxima.

"Let's talk inside, Malcolm."

~ ~ ~

Once inside the house, Brenda gave Malcolm Warren Sr. a glass of ice water and sat across from him. She tried to get control of herself and took a deep breath. "How did you find me, Malcolm?" she asked after exhaling.

"A lot of things have changed, Brenda, but some things remain the same!" Malcolm told her as he set down his now empty glass.

"So basically you had me found, didn't you?" Brenda asked him, seeing Malcolm simply nod his head yes in response. "Why doesn't that surprise me? You're still the same as always."

"Not completely the same. But you're still just as beautiful as you were when we were still together."

"That was years ago, Malcolm!"

"We're supposed to be married now, Brenda."

"Yeah! But you're forgetting you was still with your first son's mother."

Malcolm nodded his head and accepted the truth.

"Why didn't you tell me you were pregnant or that I had a son, Brenda?"

"You've seen him?" she asked.

He nodded his head again. "Let's just say he's cost me a lot of money and has caused me a lot of problems since we've heard of each other."

"Like father, like son!" Brenda replied, but then added, "I sent him to Miami almost a year ago now."

"Alone?"

"Malcolm, you don't know ReSean. That boy will survive anywhere."

"So you sent my son away because of that?" Malcolm asked, staring hard at Brenda. "That's bullshit and you know it! He may be able to survive, but you sent my son away for a reason, and I want to know why!"

"Malcolm, you can't just—!" Brenda paused in the middle of what she was saying when she heard some commotion coming from outside the house.

Brenda got up out of her seat and rushed to the front door, only for Malcolm Sr. to gently grab her and protectively pull her behind him as he pulled out his .357 from his shoulder holster under his left arm. He then opened the door and stepped out onto the front porch.

"What the hell is going on here?" James yelled as he angrily stepped past the big man who kept him from his house.

James walked up to the porch and saw a familiar-looking man in his forties, in good shape, and wearing a suit.

"Who the fuck is you?"

Malcolm ignored the man who Brenda had just told him was her husband, and simply turned to her.

"Let me take a guess, Brenda. My son was kicked out because of this piece of shit you just called your husband, wasn't he?"

"Malcolm, ReSean is a grown man!"

"But he's still your son. Our fucking son, Brenda!"

Brenda watched Malcolm turn and walk away, brushing past James, who started to say something but paused when Malcolm suddenly stopped and turned back to face Brenda.

"You wanna finish talking, I'll be in Atlanta one more night, and then I'm gone! I'm at the same hotel we last were at together," Malcolm informed her, before turning and walking out onto the sidewalk beside his car and disappearing inside once his bodyguard opened the door.

"You wanna tell me who the hell that was just now, Brenda, and why the hell he was here!" James asked his wife after the Mercedes drove off.

Brenda shook her head and looked at her husband.

"That's my son's father, Malcolm Warren!" she admitted.

"Malcolm War—! You mean the kingpin of Miami?" James asked in complete shock. "How the hell do you even know that son of a bitch?"

Brenda ignored her husband as she turned and re-entered the house, already making the decision that she was going to talk with her son's father again.

~~~

"This muthafucka!" Malcolm Sr. yelled, after hanging up the phone and leaving Malcolm Jr. another message for him to call him the minute he got the message.

"What happened?" Ike asked. "Young Malcolm not answering the phone again?"

"I'm going to really hurt that boy!" Malcolm Sr. stated as he laid his head back and sighed tiredly.
~~~

"So that's the Brenda you've told me about, huh?" Ike asked. "I see why you're still gone over her. She's a looker for a white woman, boss!"

"She's mixed!" he explained. "She's Canadian and black on her father's side, but she's Australian from her mother's side."

"Damn!" Ike replied, impressed with the combination Malcolm Sr. had just explained to him.

Ike stared at Malcolm's face and then asked, "You're still in love with her, aren't you, boss?"

Malcolm Sr. chose to ignore the question and instead told Ike he wanted to go back to the hotel. He then turned his attention back out the window while thinking not only about Brenda but also about a son he never knew he had with her.

After arriving at the hotel a little while later, both Ike and Malcolm Sr. exited the Mercedes when the valets opened their doors. Ike escorted his boss, who was extra quiet, inside the hotel.

"Boss, you okay?"

"Yeah, Ike. Just thinking!"

"Malcolm!"

Malcolm Sr. heard his name just as he walked up the elevator. He looked back and was surprised to see Brenda rushing across the hotel lobby toward him.

"I'm surprised you came straight back!" Brenda told him as she stopped in front of him. "Does your offer still stand for us to talk, Malcolm?"

"Of course, Brenda," he replied, holding out his hand to her.

He was surprised with how quickly and trustfully she placed her hand inside of his.

~~~

Malcolm Sr. reached the suite a few steps behind Ike, who held open the door for Malcolm Sr. and Brenda to enter. Malcolm Sr. then led Brenda to the sitting area.

"I see life has been really good to you," Brenda stated as she sat down on the couch and looked around the suite.

"It's been okay, but it would have been better if I had one major missing piece!" Malcolm Sr. replied, staring at Brenda.

Brenda heard his words and turned and stared directly into Malcolm's eyes. She sat a moment thinking about their past together, but quickly cleared her thoughts.

"You were right, Malcolm. ReSean and James didn't get along. They hated each other, and what made things so much harder was when James found drugs and a gun inside
~~~

ReSean's bedroom."

"What was he doing inside of ReSean's room?"

"You know, that's exactly what your son said. But the truth is that I really don't know why James was inside ReSean's bedroom," Brenda replied with a smile.

"And you never thought to question him?"

"After everything that happened, I just never thought any more about it!"

"What exactly happened, Brenda? Why did you send our son away?"

Brenda sighed loudly, and then ran her hand through her long, straight, black hair. She once again looked Malcolm in his eyes.

"ReSean and James got into a fight. ReSean not only broke James's nose, but he also pulled a gun out on him. I didn't know what else to do, Malcolm!"

"So basically you chose some guy over our son. Is that what you're telling me?" Malcolm asked, feeling his anger rising.

He stood up from beside Brenda and walked over to stand in front of the sliding glass door that led out onto the balcony. Brenda stood up and followed behind him. She gently laid her hand on his back.

"Malcolm, I'm sorry. I wasn't thinking right. I wasn't supposed to send ReSean away how I did."

"You know, in a way you sending him to Miami led him to me," Malcolm stated while staring out the glass door.

"How's he doing?"

Malcolm slowly smiled and looked over at Brenda and met her eyes. He intended to tell her that their son was doing extremely well for himself, but instead he found himself pulling Brenda up against him as their lips met together in a passion-filled kiss.

"Malcolm, we—!"

"I still love you, Brenda!" Malcolm interrupted while catching her off guard. "I've loved you all these years, and I wish I had made a different decision back then, but I won't miss out this time."

Brenda wrapped her arms and then legs around Malcolm's neck and waist after he picked her up. She found herself kissing his lips while pulling at his clothes. They were naked within minutes and lay together in his bed. Malcolm was on his back, since he knew Brenda loved to be on top and in control at the start of their love-making. She broke their kiss and for a moment just stared down into his eyes.

"I love you, Brenda," Malcolm told her as he reached up and gently brushed her hair back out of her face, before he tenderly laid his hand against the side of her face.

"I never stopped loving you, Malcolm!" Brenda admitted as she laid her cheek in his hand after missing his touch for so long.

Malcolm watched her from underneath, but he didn't say a word. He simply held her eyes as she led him into her welcoming wetness.

"Ohhh God! Yesssss!" Brenda cried out in a soft and sexy voice, feeling Malcolm's hands as they gripped her hips.

She began riding him as he balanced her above him.

"Malcolm, I missed you so much! God, I love you so much, Malcolm!"

Malcolm allowed Brenda to take control and get through her first orgasm. He missed the way she cried out his name and the way her walls gripped his manhood. Malcolm let her get through her ride, but then gently flipped her over onto her back and was rewarded with a beautiful smile.

"I want you back, Brenda!" he told her as he moved in and out of her.

"Malcolm, how? Oh God! Yesss! Baby, how are we

supposed to do that?"

"Do you trust me?"

"Malcolm, please!"

"Do you trust me?" he repeated the question, pushing deeper and causing Brenda to scream out his name. "Answer me, Brenda! Do you trust me?"

"Yesss! Oh God, yessss!" Brenda cried out as she began climaxing for the second time.

~ ~ ~

As Brenda and Malcolm lay together after their love-making, she rested her head on Malcolm's chest, playing with the hair that lightly covered the center of his chest. She then broke their silence after a few minutes.

"Malcolm, I need you to help me understand this. How are we going to work all of this with ReSean and with us? I'm sure ReSean is still upset with how I lied to him, and then last I knew you were still married to Patricia. And since I'm married to James, you've really got to help me through all of this!"

"I thought you trusted me!" Malcolm said, looking over at Brenda.

"I wouldn't be here if I didn't trust you, Malcolm."

"That's the only reason you're here?"

Brenda smiled at catching on to what he was really asking her. She then kissed him on the lips.

"I love you, too, Malcolm," Brenda admitted.

Chapter 13

MALCOLM SR. ARRIVED BACK in Miami a day later, with an agreement from Brenda that she would meet him at a specific hotel. His first stop in Miami was at his son's mansion. He watched as his son walked out the front door just as his limo pulled up in the driveway. Malcolm Sr. saw the expression on his son's face from the backseat. He then climbed out once Ike opened the door him.

"Going somewhere, boy?"

"I have a meeting to attend," Malcolm Jr. told his father with a slight attitude.

"Reschedule it!" Malcolm Sr. told him, walking off toward the mansion's front door. "We need to talk!"

Hearing the mumbling coming from his son, but planning to deal with that later as well, Malcolm Sr. stopped at the front door. A moment later, Malcolm Jr. appeared beside him, unlocking and the opening up the door. Once they were inside the house and walked into the den, Malcolm Sr. dismissed both Ike and Moses, and then he turned his attention to his son.

"Fill me in on how things having been going with Boss."

"Not really much to fill you in on," Malcolm Jr. told his

father. “I haven’t heard much from the muthafucka!”

“But I’m sure his people are still working, correct?”

“I’m planning to deal with that real soon. I’ve been recruiting new workers, and I’ve also got something else in the works as we speak!”

“Call it off!”

“What?”

“I shouldn’t have to repeat myself!” Malcolm said calmly while staring across the coffee table at his son. “I’ve come to an agreement with Boss. I do not want you fucking up business I have with him. Are we clear?”

“Wait! What do you mean you made a deal with this muthafucka?” Malcolm Jr. asked, his face showing his disbelief. “What type of deal did you make with this nigga?”

“We will discuss this when the time is right!” Malcolm Sr. told his son. He then stood up from his seat. “And if I call you any other time and you so much as allow your phone to ring once too many times, I will not call back, because I will be paying you another visit!” Malcolm Sr. explained, before he turned his back.

Malcolm Sr. motioned to Ike that they were leaving as he walked out of the den, with his son staring at him angrily.

~~~
~~~

Once they were back inside the limo and driving away from his son's mansion, Malcolm Sr. picked up his car phone. He dialed a number that he had memorized in his head, and sat listening to the line ring twice before someone answered.

"Yeah!"

"This is Malcolm."

"I know who's calling!" Boss stated. "The question is, are you calling to give me an answer to my question?"

"How about you meet me at this location, ReSean," Malcolm Sr. told him, telling Boss the address to his mansion in Miami Lakes and then hanging up immediately afterward.

"I'm pretty sure you know!" Ike stated as soon as Malcolm Sr. hung up the phone. "But you do realize that you just called your son by this real name, right?"

Smiling over at Ike, Malcolm said nothing in response. He simply looked out the window.

~~~

"What did he say?" Trigger asked as soon as Boss lowered the cell phone from his ear after talking with Malcolm Sr.

"We're meeting him to talk," Boss answered, motioning
~~~

the others to relax as they all sat inside the apartment with him at Gina's place. "I'm only taking Trigger and Black Widow with me. I don't think Malcolm is about to start the bullshit this time!"

"How can you be sure about that?" Eazy asked Boss.

"I'm going off a gut feeling right now," Boss admitted.

Boss didn't mention that it was something else Malcolm Sr. had said that had him making his decision. Boss then listened to the team complaining about his decision, but he only gave in a little and then instructed them on what he wanted done. After the instructions were announced, Trigger, Black Widow, and he all climbed into Trigger's truck and left Gina's apartment. Boss then gave Trigger directions to where they were going. He then looked over his left shoulder and heard Black Widow call his name.

"Yeah, Black! What's good?"

"You alright?"

"Yeah! Why?"

"You got this look on your face since you hung up with Malcolm Sr."

"I don't know what it is, Black. I just got this feeling that something's different. But I think I'm about to soon find out!" Boss told her, looking out his window and replaying his phone conversation while trying to pinpoint exactly what all was said that had hit something inside of him.

~ ~ ~

"Mr. Warren, sir. You have a guest," the house servant announced while Malcolm Sr. and Ike were discussing a few things businesswise.

Malcolm nodded his head in response and looked over at Ike. "See to my son!"

After Ike left the den to do as he was asked, Malcolm Sr. called out to the servant and asked for a drink to be brought to him. Moments later, Ike returned, followed by Boss and two others behind him.

"I see you've brought friends."

"I'm sure you expected that!" Boss replied, standing between Trigger and Black Widow a few feet from Malcolm.

Malcolm Sr. smirked at his son. "Do you mind if this meeting involves only the two of us? Let your friends wait with Ike while we speak," Malcolm simply asked.

Boss stared at the kingpin for a moment and then gave in and told Trigger and Black Widow to step out of the room with Ike. Once the three bodyguards had exited the room, Malcolm Sr. motioned for Boss to have a seat.

After the young man sat down across from him, Malcolm

spoke up. "Before we speak about business, Boss, let me ask you a few questions."

"You mean you still have questions even after doing your homework?" Boss asked him. "And whoever you went to for your information is good, seeing as though I'm not from Miami and very few people know my name."

Malcolm Sr. slowly smiled after realizing Boss actually did catch the use of his name on the phone earlier. Malcolm then decided to get straight to the point.

"I received information on who exactly you were from your mother, Brenda Holmes. Now Brenda Byron."

Boss maintained his cool even after hearing the bullshit that just flowed from the mouth of Malcolm. Boss slowly sat forward in his seat while smoothly pulling the butterfly knife from the arm holster Black Widow had given him on the way over.

"Give me one reason why I shouldn't end your breathing right now? How the fuck do you know my mother?"

"Because I'm your birth father!" Malcolm calmly stated, staring Boss directly in his eyes, which looked exactly like his mother's.

Boss held Malcolm's eyes, seeing the seriousness in them. He then tossed the knife onto the coffee table and then fell back in his seat.

"You're serious, aren't you?"

Instead of answering his son's question, Malcolm dug out his cell phone, hit a number on speed dial, and then hit the speaker button. After three rings, the line was answered.

"Yes, Malcolm. What's the matter?"

"Brenda, I have our son sitting here in front of me now," Malcolm informed while still staring at Boss.

"ReSean! Baby, you there?"

Boss was unable to believe what was happening. While he simply stared at the man who claimed to be his father, he recognized the voice on the phone as that of his mother. Boss then spoke up when he heard her call out to him.

"Yeah, mom! I'm here!"

"ReSean, I know you have a lot of questions, and your father and I will answer them. I will be down in Miami tomorrow night, and we will talk then. I promise."

"We'll see you tomorrow night, Brenda," Malcolm spoke up.

"Bye, Malcolm."

Malcolm hung up the phone with Brenda and then tossed the cell phone onto the coffee table. He stared at his son a few moments.

"I've thought about your offer, and I want to change it a little from what you first said."

"Keep talking," Boss told him, setting aside his feelings from what he had just learned.

"You've already taken control of the western section of Miami, so I want to give you control over the southwest as well as the south sections. There's been a little problem out in the southwest area with someone named Larry Russell."

"What about the north, east, and in-between areas?" Boss asked. "Let me guess, Malcolm Jr. runs those areas, huh?"

Malcolm caught his son's tone, even though his face showed no sign that he was upset.

"ReSean, understand something. I'm asking you to take possession of those areas because I know you're capable of dealing with that type of bullshit. Malcolm will fight, but he's lacking what I've seen you display," Malcolm explained.

"So I guess you expect me to fall for all this bullshit because I'm supposed to be your son, huh?" Boss stated with an attitude. "Hear me good, old man. I work for no man. I've been doing for me since I can remember. I ain't have no father because the muthafucka wasn't there, and my own mother chose another man—some chump husband I should have bodied—over me. So save that bullshit for that weak-ass nigga son of yours, Malcolm."

Malcolm sat back in his seat as Boss stood to his feet and left the den. Malcolm stared at the empty seat where his son had just been sitting, when Ike walked back into the room.

"Boss, everything alright?" Ike asked him.

Malcolm slowly nodded his head and then shifted his eyes up at Ike.

"Contact Malcolm Jr. and tell that boy I said to remove all his men from the southwest area. I have somebody else who's going to be taking control of that part of town."

~ ~ ~

"Boss, are you fucking serious?" Black Widow yelled in disbelief, after just listening to what Boss had to tell her and Trigger about finding out that he was the son of the legendary Malcolm Warren.

"Big bruh! So what you're telling me is that the same dude we're beefing with is actually your brother?" Trigger stated, looking from the road over at Boss with a shocked looked on his face.

"He called my mom in front of me," Boss said while he sat staring out the window. "She's supposed to come here tomorrow night so all of us can talk."

"So you didn't get Malcolm Sr. to agree to business yet?" Black Widow asked Boss.

Boss remained quiet for a moment and kept staring out the window.

"A change of plans. We're taking over the south and southwest areas of Miami!" Boss ordered.

~ ~ ~

"Hello!"

"Destiny, this is Malcolm. Has your brother called you yet?"

"No! I'm actually on my way to see him now. Why? What's happened?"

"Destiny, I want you to keep a watch on him. The boy's getting a big head, and if he don't slow down, something bad is going to happen to his ass!" Malcolm stated and then sighed loudly.

"I'm assuming you're talking about Boss, right?"

"Destiny, listen to me. I haven't told your mother or Malcolm Jr. yet, but Boss isn't the normal thug or hustler your brother may think he is. Boss is my son from another woman I used to see years ago!"

"Whoa! Wait a minute!" Destiny cried out. "What did you just say? Who's your son?"

"Destiny, you heard me. Boss is my youngest son!" Malcolm told his step-daughter.

"Oh my God!" Destiny cried in shock and disbelief. "I cannot believe this shit!"

"Just focus on what I told you!" Malcolm Sr. told her. "I don't want Malcolm Jr. doing anything stupid before I break the news to him."

After hanging up the phone with Destiny, Malcolm Sr. pulled up his youngest child's phone number because he figured he needed to talk with his daughter, Tina.

~ ~ ~

"I cannot believe this shit!" Destiny said to herself, after her father hung up the phone.

She had to pull her car over to get herself together and clear her mind. She then picked up her phone and pulled up Boss's number.

"What do you want, Destiny?" Boss answered at the start of the third ring.

"You actually answered!" she told him, but then quickly asked, "Is it true?"

"Is what true?"

"Boss, don't fucking play with me, boy! Are you fucking Malcolm's son or not?"

"So he told you," Boss said with a chuckle.

"I cannot believe this shit!" Destiny said out loud. "I'm in love with my fucking step-brother!"

"Well, now that you've shared that bit of information, how about telling me what exactly you want, Destiny! I've got things to do."

"Boss, I need to see you," Destiny begged.

"Bye, Destiny."

"Boss!" Destiny cried.

But after hearing nothing but dead silence, she looked at the screen and saw that Boss had hung up the phone.

"Damn it!"

Chapter 14

BRENDA HAD MIXED FEELINGS as she pulled her rented Lexus truck into the parking lot of the hotel at which Malcolm had asked her to meet him. She was not only thinking about the strong feelings she had again for Malcolm, but also about her son. Brenda found a place to park in front of the hotel's entrance. After shutting off the engine, she grabbed her purse and overnight bag she had packed for the trip.

Brenda locked up the Lexus and then walked into the five-star hotel. Per Malcolm's instructions, she stopped at the front desk and picked up her keys to a penthouse suite under her name that was paid in full for three weeks. She took the elevator up to the top floor and then got off. She keyed into the luxuriously furnished suite and could only smile, when she reminded herself that Malcolm always had great style.

She set down her bags and then pulled out her phone to call Malcolm.

"Hello, sweetheart."

"Hello, Malcolm. Where are you?" Brenda said, smiling even wider at the greeting.

"Are you at the hotel yet?"

"That's where I'm standing now. Where are you?"

"Three minutes away. I'll see you in a few minutes."

Brenda was still smiling and shaking her head after Malcolm hung up the phone. She found herself rushing to quickly change clothes and get freshened up before he arrived at her suite. Within three minutes, she changed into jeans, and a blouse that she knew hugged her C-cup breasts, which she knew Malcolm loved her to show off. She was just having a seat in the sitting room when the suite door opened, drawing her attention as Malcolm stepped into the room.

"Why am I not surprised you also have a key?" Brenda said, smiling as she stood back up from her seat as he walked over and wrapped his still thick and strong arms around her.

"I've missed you!" he told Brenda before kissing her passionately.

"Wow!" Brenda said breathlessly. "You really must have missed me!"

"So how are we going to do this with ReSean, Malcolm? I know he's upset with me for lying to him," Brenda asked after they sat down together.

"He's barely speaking to me after I told him I am his

father," Malcolm explained. "But he should be here in a little while. I spoke with him, and he agreed to meet us here."

"Where is he?"

"He was with his son and sister."

"What?" Brenda cried out. "What do you mean his son? ReSean has a son already, Malcolm?"

"Relax, Brenda!" Malcolm told her with a smile. "The young boy is ReSean's adoptive son."

"Oh my God!" Brenda said in shock. "My baby adopted a baby."

Malcolm then heard his phone ring while smiling at Brenda. He dug out his phone and then glanced at the screen. "Yes, Ike?"

"ReSean's on his way up, boss."

"All right!" Malcolm replied, before hanging up the phone.

He then looked back at Brenda and said, "ReSean's on his way up now."

~~~

Boss stepped off the elevator on the top floor. He glanced around as he walked over to the suite's door. He knocked but continued to look around. He was impressed with the style of the hotel.
~~~

Boss heard the door being unlocked and watched as it slowly opened. He stood staring at his mother, who stood there smiling at him as tears began to fall from her eyes.

"Oh my baby!" Brenda cried, rushing over to her son, throwing her arms around him in a hug, and then leaning into him. "ReSean, I'm sorry, sweetheart. I'm so sorry!"

Boss returned his mother's hug even though he was still feeling a certain way about how she had lied to him and sent him away with nothing. He kissed the top of her head, which caused her to smile up at him.

"Come on! Your father's already inside waiting on us!" Brenda told her son, leading Boss inside the suite by his hand.

~~~

"Hello!"

"Brandi, it's Destiny."

"You're finally calling me? So what's up? You and Malcolm ready to do this?"

"So you're still willing to help us with getting rid of Boss?"

"Of course," Brandi answered. "But I want something in return."

"What's that?" Destiny asked, with a loud sigh.
~~~

"I want that bitch Vanity. I can't stand that ho!" Brandi answered, ignoring the sigh from the spoiled rich bitch.

"How exactly do you expect us to find her? Boss keeps that girl hid off somewhere."

"Well I guess it's our lucky day since I just found out she bought the old club we used to dance at called the Pink Palace."

"Pink Palace, huh?" Destiny repeated. "I'll talk to Malcolm about it. But are you still willing to help us get rid of Boss?"

"Just call me when you guys are ready. I'll be ready too!" Brandi told her, hanging up afterward.

~ ~ ~

Boss sat down with his mother and the man she told him was his birth father. He listened as the two of them broke down what they swore was the true history of how Boss came about and why he never knew his father. Boss sat quietly while taking in everything the two of them had to say.

"What now?" Boss asked, when they were finished with their story.

"What do you mean, what now, ReSean?" Brenda asked with confusion.

"I mean, I'm turning twenty-two in a few months. And for twenty of those years I didn't have a father, and for one of those years I didn't have a mother. So what's the point now? One didn't even know of me, and the other didn't give a fuck about me!"

"ReSean!" Brenda cried in shock. "Honey, that isn't true! I just made a bad decision, but you know I love you. I can't take back what I did, but I really am sorry."

"I bet!" Boss stated, before standing from his seat and starting toward the door.

"ReSean!" Brenda cried out to him again, only to be ignored.

"Boss!" Malcolm yelled with a voice booming throughout the penthouse as his son paused at the door.

Malcolm stood up beside Brenda and walked over to the door where Boss stood with his back to him.

"So you're just going to walk out on your mother, boy?"

Boss turned and faced Malcolm and met his eyes directly.

"Who was there for me when I needed them?" Boss questioned.

"The same woman you're about to walk out on!" Malcolm told his son in a calmer voice. "Yes, she may have missed one year of your life because of a decision she made, but let's be men right now. Was she not there when you needed her growing up? Tell me something; how many times did you fuck up and get locked up or do something stupid growing up and your mom was there, right or wrong, holding and backing up your ass? Now she messes up once and you're ready to just cut her completely off! What type of man does that make you?"

Boss stared directly into Malcolm's eyes. He was unable to really ignore what the man was saying, since it was the truth.

"So I guess now you're supposed to be my father making up for lost time," Boss said.

Malcolm stepped aside as Boss walked past him and headed back to sit down beside his mother. Malcolm smirked and shook his head as he followed his son back over to sit down on the opposite side of this mother.

~~~

Malcolm Jr. watched the Dodge Charger as it slowly pulled up alongside the G-Wagon, only to continue passing it and then park in front of his Benz. Detective Larry Sumner climbed out of the Charger and headed in the direction of the Mercedes. Malcolm Jr. told his bodyguard, Moses, to unlock
~~~

the door as the detective climbed inside.

"Malcolm Warren Jr.," Detective Sumner stated, smirking at the young son of the legendary Malcolm Warren Sr. "I'm very surprised I received a call from you, Junior. What can I do for you?"

"I have a job for you," Malcolm Jr. told the detective.

"I don't remember putting the word out that I was looking for work; and from what I've been hearing, anybody who messes with you ends up dead! I hear this new guy Boss is taking over things now!" Detective Sumner interrupted him.

"Mutha—!" Malcolm started, but caught himself and calmed down. "I'm not worried about this weak-ass, self-proclaimed Boss! I'm paying you $60,000 to lock his ass up for a really long fucking time!"

"How exactly am I supposed to do that?" Detective Sumner asked.

"I have somebody who's willing to testify that Boss was the person who killed Detective Howard Shaw as well as Detective Corey Davis."

The detective stared at the son of the legendary Malcolm Warren Sr. and saw no similarity of the legend in the boy sitting across from him.

"Did this witness see this actually happen?"

"Does it really matter?" Malcolm Jr. asked, shooting the detective a hard look.

"I figured!" Detective Sumner replied. "So when do you want me to start with this case against Boss?"

Malcolm Jr. tossed a black leather tote bag into the detective's lap.

"There's your money! I want this muthafucka off the streets no later than tomorrow night!"

Detective Sumner looked from Malcolm Jr. down to the money in his lap, picked up the bag, and then climbed back out of the G-Wagon.

Chapter 15

MALCOLM HEARD THE RINGING phone a few minutes after Brenda began nudging him in his side and calling out his name. Malcolm rolled over and pulled Brenda in against his chest, catching the soft moan she released before wrapping her arm around him.

"Malcolm, can you please answer that phone?" Brenda said against his chest. "It's been ringing nonstop for the last ten minutes!"

Malcolm sighed as he released Brenda and rolled back on his left side to pick up the phone. He answered without checking to see who was calling. "Yeah! Who's this?"

Malcolm heard an automatic recording asking if he wanted to accept a collect call from a ReSean Holmes. Malcolm shot up into a sitting position after hearing his son's name and also that he was in jail. Malcolm accepted the call and waited a brief moment as the call was processed.

"ReSean, what the hell are you doing in jail?"

"What?" Brenda screamed as she shot straight up in bed and looked questioningly over at Malcolm.

"I don't know what the fuck is going on! I just got snatched up this morning out of my fucking bed about some murder," Boss explained.

"Who did they say you killed?"

"What?" Brenda yelled again, staring hard at Malcolm and wanting answers.

Malcolm motioned for Brenda to hold on, and then told Boss not to say anything else on the phone. He then told him that his lawyer would be there in a bit. After hanging up with Boss, Malcolm instantly pulled up his defense attorney's number, just as Brenda started questioning him about Boss.

"I'll explain in a minute, Brenda," Malcolm told her, just as the attorney picked up the ringing line.

~ ~ ~

After hanging up the phone with his father more than twenty minutes again, Boss sat inside his cell and heard his name called over the dormitory-style jail unit speaker, telling him to report to the officer station. He swung his legs out of his bunk, stood up, and then left the cell.

Boss's cell was on the bottom floor but in the far right corner. He made his way to the front of the unit and ignored the stares from a few of the inmates inside the day room as he walked by. Once he arrived at the officer station and knocked on the door, he waited a moment until the door opened.

"You Holmes?" the male officer asked, looking Boss over.

"Yeah!"

"You got an attorney visit. They'll be here to pick you up in a few minutes."

"A'ight!" Boss replied.

He was just about to turn and walk away when he heard, "So you the one they call Boss, huh?"

Boss looked over his shoulder at the guard looking him over. Boss turned back to face the guard and was just about to say something, when the unit door was pulled open and a female officer entered the unit.

"Officer Gills, is this the inmate for the attorney visit?" the female officer asked while looking Boss over.

"Yeah!" Boss answered as he started toward the door.

Boss left the unit and was really not up for friendly conversation with the flirting escorting female guard. He ignored her most of the way until they reached the room in which he would be meeting with his attorney. The female guard then read him the rules and asked if he understood how things went.

"Yeah, I got it!" Boss replied to her questioning before turning away from her and entering the room.

Boss sat down at one of the two seats at the metal table and waited a little over eight minutes, when another door opened. In walked a very young-looking, medium-height, brown-skinned woman wearing a navy-blue pantsuit.

"Hello, ReSean. I'm your attorney, Ms. Faith Summers," the attorney introduced herself, setting down her snakeskin briefcase before holding out her hand to shake his.

"Malcolm sent you?" Boss asked, shaking the attorney's hand. "You look really young to be an attorney."

"If you consider thirty-five years old young, then thank you!" she told Boss as she sat down across from him at the table. "So how about we get down to business, ReSean? You're charged with two counts of capital murder of two police officers, as well as manslaughter on a Mrs. Pamela Shaw."

"Bullshit!" Boss stated, and said nothing more.

"ReSean, there's a witness!" she told him. "This witness is willing to come forward and testify that they witnessed you murder—!"

"Who's this witness?" Boss demanded, cutting off his attorney.

"I won't know until later in the case, ReSean. I can see if the district attorney will put a rush on things, but we won't really know much more than we do know now unless this case goes to trial."

"I don't plan on having that!" Boss said, mumbling to himself as he began trying to put something together inside his head.

~ ~ ~

Boss finished up with the attorney thirty minutes later and was escorted back to his unit. He went directly to the phone area and first called Vanity.

Once she answered the phone and then accepted the call, she wasted no time questioning Boss on how he was doing.

"Ma, I'm good. But I need you to do me a favor."

"What is it, babe?"

"Put Trigger on a three-way."

"He's right here. Hold on."

Boss waited a brief moment before he heard his boy on the line.

"Yeah! What's up, big bruh?"

"Baby bruh, I'm a need you to come out here to check me out with Vanity. I got some shit that needs to be done because games are being played, and we both know who's behind this shit!"

"Say no more! I'm there whenever big sis gets out there."

"That's what's up!" Boss stated, before he continued, "Tell Eazy and the rest of the team to expect my call real soon."

"I got you, big bruh."

"A'ight. Put Vanity back on the phone. I'ma get at you later, baby bruh."

Boss waited a brief minute while the phone was exchanged. He glanced around the unit, just as Vanity came back on the line.

"Yeah, babe!"

"What's good, ma? You alright?"

"I should be asking you that. I hate that you're not here."

"No worries and no pressure, ma. I'll be home soon."

"What's really going on, Boss?"

"I'll explain everything when you come out here, but I need you to three-way Malcolm on the phone."

"You mean your father?"

"Yeah, him, Vanity!"

"Hold on!"

Boss waited as Vanity connected the three-way call with his father. Boss then glanced around again, and like last time, he caught some slim, light-skinned dude watching him. He looked away when their eyes met for a brief moment.

"Babe, you there?" Vanity asked as she came back on the line.

"Yeah, ma! I'm here!" Boss replied when he heard the line ring.

"Hello!" Malcolm Sr. answered after two rings.

"Malcolm, it's Boss!"

"Did the attorney come?"

"Yeah. I spoke with her, and she's talking about capital murder and manslaughter charges on two cops and some woman."

"What's your bond?"

"I don't get one with the capital murder charges!"

"Damn it!" Malcolm yelled. "Who was the arresting officer?"

"Dude named Larry Sumner," Boss stated. "The attorney also said there's a witness who supposedly saw the whole murder and is willing to talk!"

"Let me get on the phone and make a few calls. Call your mother's phone because she wants to talk to you."

~ ~ ~

Malcolm Sr. hung up with his son and then kept his word. He made a few calls while Brenda spoke with Boss on the phone. After about ten minutes, he not only had the number but also the home address of Detective Sergeant Larry Sumner. Malcolm found the information he was looking for after only a few phone calls. He then interrupted Brenda's conversation and explained that he would be back and that he had to go handle something.

Malcolm Sr. left the suite and found Ike waiting for him downstairs inside the hotel lobby. Malcolm was then escorted outside to a team of twenty men waiting for him.

"Where we going, boss?" Ike asked, once they were inside the back of the limo.

Malcolm handed Ike a piece of paper with the address and phone number of Detective Sumner.

"We need to have a talk with the detective about the arrest of my son," Malcolm explained to him.

~~~

Detective Sumner stepped out of the shower and heard his phone ringing, just as he was trying to dry off. He walked naked from the bathroom into his bedroom and snatched up his ringing cell phone.

"Who the hell is this?" the detective barked into the phone.

"You have two minutes to get outside or you'll have visitors."
~~~

"Who the hell is this?" the detective yelled after hearing the demands, only to hear silence now.

The detective looked at his phone and saw that the caller had hung up. He tossed the phone onto the bed and waved off the call as he turned back to getting dressed.

Two minutes later, just as he was sitting down on his bed dressed in gray cotton sweatpants and a white wifebeater, a hulk-like man walked into his bedroom. He was followed by two armed men.

"What in the hell is this?"

"You have visitors," Ike told the detective, just as the two guys approached him, grabbed him by the arms, and began roughly escorting him from the bedroom.

The detective put up a mild fight while trying to figure out exactly who the men inside his house were, as well as how they even got inside. Detective Sumner got his answer once he stepped into the front room and saw none other than Malcolm Warren Sr., the legend himself.

"Detective Larry Sumner?" Malcolm Sr. shouted while looking the detective over. "Why don't you have a seat! We have much to talk about."

As the detective was forcefully seated on the sofa directly across from the kingpin, he decided not to play games with the legend. He wanted to get to the reason he was sitting in his living room with Malcolm Warren.

"Look! Your son contacted me, alright? He wanted this guy Boss off the streets, and he paid me a lot of money to do it for him. I just did what I was paid to do. That's it!"

"So my son paid you to arrest Boss, right?"

"That's the full of it!" the detective admitted.

Malcolm Sr. nodded his head slowly at the detective's confession and then said, "So tell me, Detective Sumner, who exactly is this witness who's supposedly testifying against Boss?"

"I don't know that exactly," the detective confessed. "Your son didn't tell me that!"

"Well, Detective," Malcolm said in a louder voice. "I think you need to figure out a way to find out, and I need to know in the next ten minutes."

~ ~ ~

Malcolm Sr. waited and allowed Detective Sumner to do whatever it was he needed to do, until he came back with the name of the witness. After receiving the information he wanted, Malcolm left the detective's house and immediately got on the phone and called his son.

"Yeah!" Malcolm Jr. answered at the start of the second

ring, sounding as if he had an attitude.

"Boy, who the hell is Brandi Wyatts?" Malcolm Sr. barked into the phone as soon as he heard his son's voice.

Malcolm Jr. remained quiet for a moment, since he was a bit surprised at what he just heard his father ask. "She's who's helping us with our problem. I told you I would handle it," he explained to his father.

"Boy, are you that fucking stupid?" Malcolm yelled into the phone. "I'm pretty fucking sure that I clearly told you not to fuck with Boss, didn't I, boy?"

"But I thought—!"

"That's your problem: you keep fucking thinking and not fucking listening!" Malcolm Sr. screamed. "I don't give a fuck what you do, but you better fix this shit, and I mean fast!"

~~~

Malcolm Jr. heard his father rant and rave like never before, before hanging up on him. Malcolm Jr. was more confused than ever at the way his father was reacting to dealing with their problem.

"Let me guess!" Destiny spoke up, seeing her step-brother was done on the phone with their father. "Malcolm went off about Boss being in jail, didn't he?"
~~~

"I don't understand that just now!" Malcolm Jr. told his step-sister. "He sounded more upset that Boss was in jail than over me ignoring his order to leave Boss alone. I just don't fucking get that!"

"Maybe Malcolm has his reasons."

"Some bullshit about some business deal the two of them agreed on."

"Business deal, huh?"

Malcolm Jr. looked over at Destiny and the way she was acting, and noticed the look on her face. He knew something was up!

"What the hell do you know, Destiny?"

"Noth—!"

"Don't fucking lie to me!" Malcolm Jr. shouted through hard-pressed lips. "Tell me what the fuck you know, now!"

Destiny sighed and shook her head, since she already knew her step-brother was about to cut a fool. She still told him what he wanted to know. "Malcolm is acting this way because he just found out Boss is really his son."

Malcolm Jr. stared at Destiny after hearing what she had just told him. After processing it, he finally exploded. "What the fuck are you talking about? Who told you that bullshit?"

"Malcolm did!" she added. "He called me and admitted

that to me after telling me to watch you and make sure you didn't do anything stupid like this!"

"This is some bullshit!" Malcolm Jr. yelled as he began pacing and talking to himself, unable to really believe what Destiny had just revealed to him.

"What did Malcolm say?" Destiny asked, interrupting her step-brother.

"Fuck what Malcolm said!" he replied, with spit flying from his mouth with every word he spoke. "Fuck that bitch-ass nigga Boss too! I'm tired of listening to his ass! This is my fucking city, and I've been running it too long to let Malcolm or this bitch-ass nigga Boss take what's mine. Fuck 'em both!"

Destiny shook her head while watching her step-brother's response to what she just told him. She could already see the problem that was growing, not only with her step-brother and step-father, but also with Boss and Malcolm Jr.

Chapter 16

BOSS HAD APPEARED BEFORE a judge four times before he was finally released and his charges were dismissed. The DA no longer had a witness and really had nothing else to go on to get a conviction against him. Boss walked out of the Dade County Jail seven hours later and was met by his woman, who was screaming excitedly.

"Oh, babe! I missed you so much!" Vanity cried before she passionately kissed her man.

Boss pulled out of the kiss once he felt Vanity press into him with a soft moan escaping from her lips. He smiled down into her eyes, only to catch movement to the side. He looked over and saw his mother and father standing a few feet away smiling at them.

"Come on!" Vanity said, smiling as she led Boss over to his parents.

"My baby!" Brenda cried as she threw her arms around her son's waist. "I'm so happy you're out of that place, ReSean!"

Boss kissed the top of his mother's head while he held her wrapped in his right arm. He then lifted his eyes to meet Malcolm Sr.'s eyes.

"How'd you do it?" Boss inquired.

"I did what I needed to do to free my son. Period!" Malcolm told his son as the two of them stood staring each other in the eyes, until Boss made the first move.

He released his mother, and then stepped toward his father and surprised him with an embrace.

"Thanks!" Boss said as he hugged his father for the first time ever.

"Ummm, excuse me!" Boss heard someone say.

Boss looked past his father after releasing him, only to see Trigger, Eazy, and the rest of his crew.

"You do got other family members out here, you know. Show some love, big bruh!" Trigger continued.

Boss smiled as he walked over to his crew and was greeted with hugs and even kisses from Princess and Black Widow.

After the hugs were finished, Malcolm Sr. pulled Boss off to the side. "I want you to ride with me. I wanna talk to you about something."

Boss nodded his head in agreement and then looked back at his mother and Vanity. They were being escorted to her Land Rover by Princess and Black Widow. He peeped Trigger and Ike talking with each other but still watching the women.

"Come on!" Malcolm said, nodding for Boss to follow him over to the limo.

Once they were in the backseat of the limo, both Ike and Trigger climbed inside with them, and Malcolm then looked over at Boss.

"ReSean, look! I can't change the past and my not being there as your father, but I am man enough to ask you now to let me have the chance to be a father or at least a friend and get to know you."

"I can't find a reason why not!" Boss said, nodding his head and smirking.

Malcolm smiled when he heard his son's response.

"Now, there's one more thing I wanna talk to you about."

"What's that?"

"I know you've put in a lot of work out here in Miami and whatnot, but I don't want to see you and your brother getting—!"

"You mean Malcolm, right?" Boss asked, correcting his father.

Malcolm was unable to stop smiling at his son's quick attitude change. Malcolm Sr. ignored the problem between his sons for the moment, so he went ahead and continued what he was just saying. "I'm pretty sure you've got a lot going on down here, but I need you back in Chicago. I'm dealing with a lot out there, and I need a little help getting things in order."

"You need me?" Boss asked, smirking as he gave his father a look of disbelief. "Come on! The legendary Malcolm Warren Sr. needs me?"

"Boy, do I have to repeat my request?" Malcolm asked with a smirk while holding his son's eyes.

Boss was certain why his father was requesting what he was.

"So how long do we have to be out there? I do have businesses I need to deal with!" Boss chuckled.

"We leave in three days," Malcolm informed his son. "My advice is to take only a few of your strongest team members but leave behind someone who's capable of running things until your return."

Boss nodded his head at his father's words of advice. He then shifted his eyes over at Trigger, who he was not surprised to see was watching and paying attention to everything Boss and his father were discussing. Trigger then received a strong nod, only to return it knowingly.

~~~
~~~

Once they returned to the penthouse in which Boss, Vanity, and Lloyd lived, everyone crowded inside. The new servant Vanity had just hired brought everyone drinks. Boss then took the time to discuss with his team what he and his father had spoken about on the way home from jail.

"So who's all going and who's staying?" Butter asked, speaking up once Boss was finished talking.

Boss slowly nodded his head at the question Butter had just asked. He then looked over at Eazy. "E, I want you to hold things down while I'm up in Chicago with Malcolm. Butter, Magic, Rico, and Black Widow will stay with Eazy. Savage, Joker, Trigger, and Princess are coming with me and Vanity."

"Ummm!" Vanity spoke up. "Babe, I think I should stay here. I'm in the middle of getting things together for the club, and I just can't up and leave right now."

"Can't—!" Boss started, but paused from what he was about to say. "Black Widow, then you're switching with Princess and coming with me to Chicago. Princess, you know what I expect from you."

"Relax, pretty boy," Princess told Boss, smiling at him and winking her eye. "I got it under control."

Boss continued to discuss plans and whatnot with the

crew. He then made sure the team understood what was going on, and then both he and Malcolm broke away from the others and walked out onto the private 1,600-square-foot roof-top terrace with a kitchen.

The two decided to grab a drink. Boss chose a Heineken, while Malcolm decided on a Jack Daniels. They stood staring out over the water and the city.

"So who'd you pay to get the charges dropped?" Boss asked, after a few minutes of no one saying anything.

"I had the mayor take care of your case for me," Malcolm answered while continuing to stare out over the city.

"Who was the witness?" Boss asked as he took a sip of beer and focused on the water as his mind wandered.

"Someone named Wyatts. Brandi Wyatts," Malcolm told his son.

Malcolm instantly noticed the way Boss looked at him.

"Let me guess, you know this person?"

"Yeah! We've had dealings once before," Boss chuckled softly after shaking his head.

"I see!" Malcolm stated, actually understanding what his son meant.

"Let me ask you something," Boss began, getting his father's attention once more. "Are you asking me to come to

Chicago for business or to deal with problems?"

"Business!" Malcolm answered, before adding a moment later, "And maybe a problem if it leads to it."

Boss nodded his head in understanding.

"A'ight. I'm cool with all this you got going on, but just so we're clear, I plan on expanding my own business since I'll be out of state."

"You mean those Blue Devils of yours?" Malcolm asked him.

"Pretty much," Boss replied. "I see an opportunity to expand my business the same way you have. I'll respect your business, but do I have your okay to build mine?"

Malcolm slowly smirked at his son's business mind-set. He then dropped his arm across Boss's shoulders and pulled him in close. "I wouldn't have it any other way, son."

"This is beautiful," both Malcolm and Boss heard.

They looked behind them and saw Vanity and Brenda walking out onto the rooftop.

Malcolm smiled as he released his son and accepted Brenda in his arms. Malcolm then kissed her lips, only to hear someone loudly clear his throat.

"Somebody wanna tell me what's up?" Boss asked, staring at his parents while Vanity hugged into him.

"We'll discuss this later, ReSean!" Brenda told him, with a smile on her face. "Why don't we all go back inside with the others, since the food should be here soon."

As Boss allowed Vanity to pull him into the penthouse, he looked back at his parents as they followed behind whispering to each other and softly laughing. Boss made sure to keep in mind to ask his father just what was going on with his mother.

Once they were all back inside, the food had arrived. Ms. Harris, the house servant, already had most of Boss's crew eating, along with Malcolm's personal bodyguard, Ike. Boss found a spot for him and Vanity next to Lloyd. Boss rubbed the back of his son's head, and then winked at him once he looked up from his food.

"Me and Vanity wanna talk to you later about everything that's going on, alright, lil' man?"

Lloyd nodded his head in response and turned back to his food as Vanity kissed him on the cheek.

Chapter 17

BOSS LEFT MIAMI ON his father's private jet and landed in Chicago a few minutes after midnight on a private landing strip. They were met by Malcolm's security team along with a Rolls-Royce Wraith and three Mercedes-Benz GL 63 trucks. Boss followed his father over to the Wraith along with Trigger. At his father's suggestion, he motioned for Black Widow and the others to take one of the Benz trucks. While Ike drove with Trigger next to him in front, Boss sat next to his father in the backseat of the car. Boss then turned to Malcolm when he heard his father call out his name.

"Yeah! What's up?"

"I called ahead and had things set up for you and your people," Malcolm explained to him. "It's a place not too far from the mansion. We're headed there now, and later in the day we can meet and discuss business."

Boss simply nodded his head after what his father had just explained to him. He then turned his attention back out the window, sightseeing as well as thinking about his family back in Miami. Once the Wraith pulled up in front of the guarded gate to a high-rise apartment building, Boss looked over at Malcolm as Ike was pulling into the front gate.

"This where you got us at?"

"Is there a problem?" Malcolm asked, shifting his eyes over to Boss.

"Naw!" Boss answered.

He was actually surprised at how his father was hooking up him and his team.

~ ~ ~

After Ike parked inside the private parking garage along with the Benz truck Black Widow and the others were riding in, Boss, Malcolm, Ike, and Trigger started toward the elevator, waiting a minute for Black Widow, Savage, and Joker.

They rode the elevator up to the top floor of the building and then followed Malcolm and Ike when they stepped out. Boss paid attention as his father explained that the penthouse was two properties he had combined that comprised 4,500 square feet. The place had five spacious bedrooms and 5.5 baths, and it overlooked the lake from five different terraces. Once they were inside the penthouse, Boss was able to see the enormous, open entertainment area and the huge state-of-the-art kitchen, marble floors, and venetian plaster throughout.

"So, what do you think?" Malcolm asked, looking

around at his son.

"Yo, Boss!" Joker spoke up, drawing everyone's attention to him. "This is what's up, big homie! Your pops is showing us crazy love with this right here!"

Boss shook his head and smirked at Joker as he turned around and looked back at his father.

"I guess you got your answer!"

Malcolm nodded his head in approval and then handed over the keys to the penthouse.

"The truck is yours until we can pick you up something else. I'll see you later in the day," Malcolm explained.

Boss walked his father to the door and was caught off guard when he received an embrace and a kiss on the side of his forehead from his father.

"Thanks for coming, Son. I'll see you later, ReSean," Malcolm said, with Boss nodding his head in understanding.

~ ~ ~

Vanity was unable to get fully back to sleep after Boss, Trigger, and the others had left with Malcolm to drive out to the airstrip. Vanity lay in bed watching the news with no sound, but she was really just waiting until Gigi called her.

Vanity heard a soft knock at her bedroom door. She called out that the door was open, and she smiled when

Lloyd walked inside.

"You sleeping?" Lloyd asked near the door.

"No, man!" Vanity answered. "What's up? You okay?"

"Yeah! I just wanted to ask you something."

"What's wrong?"

"Well, I was wondering, since summer starts next week, do you think Tina could spend the summer here with us?"

"Here with us, huh?" Vanity asked, smiling at Lloyd. "Man, I don't mind if Tina spends the summer with us, but she's going to have to ask her mother first."

"She already did," Lloyd admitted, smiling at Vanity. "She's waiting on you to call so she can talk to you."

Vanity smiled as she lay back watching Lloyd leave the bedroom. She shook her head noticing how much he was becoming like Boss. She focused her attention on her phone once it began ringing from over on the bedside table. Vanity noticed the Chicago area code and smiled when she realized who was calling, so she answered the call.

"Hey, babe! I see you all made it to Chicago."

"Yeah! A little while ago," Boss told her. "You miss me yet?"

"You miss me, nigga?"

"Tell me something. How is it possible that you can

answer a question with another question?"

"Shut up, boy!" Vanity told him, laughing at Boss. "You know I miss you, babe."

"That's a little better!" Boss responded with a chuckle. "I miss you too, ma. But I want you to be careful while I'm gone, and Princess is to go everywhere with you. Are we clear?"

"Yes, boy!" Vanity said, sucking her teeth while smiling.

Vanity continued her phone call with Boss until Gigi's phone call came in. Vanity told Boss she needed to get up and start getting ready, since Gigi was finally calling.

"Just hit me up later!" Boss told Vanity, letting her know the number he was calling from was to the penthouse and that his phone still worked.

"I love you!" Vanity told Boss, smiling after hearing him say it back.

After hanging up with Boss, Vanity called Gigi back. She then climbed out of bed just as Gigi answered the phone.

"What took you so long?"

"I was on the phone with my babe," Vanity explained to Gigi as she walked into the bathroom. "They made it to Chicago."

"You ain't talk to my boo?" Gigi asked her.

"Naw, girl!" Vanity answered. "Boss said the others were getting ready for bed. There's a time change between here and there, girl. But I'm sure Trigger's ass is gonna call."

"He better!" Gigi exclaimed while sucking her teeth. "Anyways, I'm down the street from the penthouse now. Is you ready?"

"I will be when you get here. So let's go, girl! I still gotta call Princess and see where she's at. Bye."

After hanging up, Vanity began to dial Princess's phone number.

Chapter 18

BOSS WAS UP EARLY even after getting to sleep only a few hours ago after arriving in Chicago. He was now standing out on the terrace of the new penthouse that his father had actually bought for him. He heard the sliding glass door open behind him. He then looked over his shoulder and saw Trigger walk outside. Boss gave a nod of the head to his boy as Trigger stepped up beside him.

"What's up, big bruh?" Trigger asked as he began lighting up a rolled joint that was meant for the two of them.

"I'm surprised you're up already," Boss told Trigger, cutting his eyes over to him.

"Shit on my mind!" Trigger told Boss. "I never really got to sleep, but I was just relaxing and thinking."

"Can anyone join this party?" Black Widow asked as she also joined Boss and Trigger out on the terrace.

Boss took the blunt from Trigger as Black Widow stepped up beside him on his left.

"What are you doing up, Black?" Boss asked her.

"New state and can't sleep, so here I am!" Black Widow explained, before she questioned why both of them were still up as well.

"Too much on the brain," Trigger answered.

"Money on the brain!" Boss stated, causing both Trigger and Black Widow to laugh lightly, even though he was dead-ass serious.

"So, what time are we supposed to be hooking up with your dad?" Black Widow asked Boss while taking the blunt he held out for her.

Boss looked down at his square-faced Kenneth Cole rose-gold watch and checked the time. Boss then went ahead and dug out his phone and pulled up the number his father had given to him.

While Boss listened to the line ring, he passed the blunt back over to Trigger from Black Widow, just as his father's line answered.

"Hello."

Boss was caught off guard for a brief moment when an unfamiliar voice answered, but then he remembered his father's wife.

"Good morning. Is Malcolm Warren Sr. around?"

"Who's calling?"

"Can you tell him ReSean's on the phone, please."

"Just a moment, please."

Boss shook his head at the fact that he just spoke with his

father's wife. Boss then stared out over the water and was thinking about the kiss his mother and father had shared before leaving for Chicago.

"ReSean!"

Boss heard his father's voice and lost his train of thought. He then focused back on the phone call. "Yeah, I'm here!"

"I'm surprised you're up so early," Malcolm told Boss.

"Money's being moved; and if I ain't got a hand in the movement, then something ain't right in the world!" Boss stated to his father. "So what's up? What are we doing today?"

"Give me twenty minutes and I'll be at your place."

"Twenty minutes," Boss repeated before hanging up with his father.

"What did Malcolm say?" Black Widow asked as soon as Boss lowered the phone from his ear.

"Twenty minutes," Boss told her. "Go ahead and wake up Savage and Joker."

~~~

Boss heard the elevator once it reached the top floor, just as he was exiting the kitchen. Boss unlocked and opened the door just a crack, which was enough to be seen. He then headed into the den where the others were eating breakfast.
~~~

"ReSean!" Malcolm called out after entering the penthouse behind Ike.

"We're in the den," Boss called out in response.

A few moments later, Boss saw Ike and then his father walk into the den.

"You guys hungry?"

"We ate," Malcolm replied, nodding in approval at seeing the way that his son and his crew all ate together. "After you're finished, we leave!"

"Where are we going?" Boss asked as he stuck a mouthful of eggs with cheese into his mouth.

"We spoke about this on the morning before I left," Malcolm mentioned. "We're meeting a friend to get you and your friends some transportation, and then I want to take you around to see a little of Chicago. But we have a meeting at noon and another one at 2:15."

Boss nodded his head while he continued to eat his breakfast. But he still listened to what his father had to say. Boss stood up from his seat while still eating and then started walking toward the den's entrance. As he was walking, his father spoke up. "Where are you going?"

"I'm finished eating. Let's get going!" Boss said as he walked out the den door.

Malcolm smirked while watching his son. He then noticed that Trigger, the women, and the other two men all followed behind Boss, leaving their plates filled with food.

~ ~ ~

Ten minutes later, Boss was seated inside the backseat of his father's Maybach, with Trigger up front with Ike. Boss sat discussing different business topics with his father. Before he even realized it, they were pulling up in front of a big, wide warehouse.

"What's this place?" Boss asked as Ike blew the car horn.

"It's where we're meeting my friend," Malcolm told his son, just as the warehouse doors began to slide open and Ike began slowly pulling inside.

"Get the fuck outta here!" Boss said to himself as he took in what he was seeing.

Malcolm looked to his son, saw the look on his face, and then chucked. He then climbed from the car once Ike had parked and opened the car door for him.

"My friend, Warren!" Darrell Stevenson said, smiling as he approached Malcolm.

Boss watched his father embrace the white man who looked to be in his late thirties or early forties. Boss caught the name Stevenson from his father, just as Malcolm motioned for him to come over.

"Darrell Stevenson, I want you to meet my son I was telling you about," Malcolm introduced as he proudly looked over at Boss. "ReSean, this is my good friend, Darrell Stevenson."

"The youngest Warren!" Stevenson commented with a smile as he looked the boy over. "So, you're Brenda's boy, huh?"

"Stevenson grew up with me, ReSean," Malcolm told Boss. "He knows your mother as well."

"He looks just like you, Warren," Stevenson said, still staring at Boss.

Boss then introduced Trigger, Black Widow, Savage, and Joker to Stevenson.

"Stevenson, I want my son and his friends all to pick out something to drive, and do you have any protection for them?" Malcolm inquired.

"It's what I do!" Stevenson stated, smiling at his oldest and best friend.

~~~

Boss looked around the warehouse at all the different styles of cars, SUVs, trucks, and even some motorcycles. But Boss was surprised that he didn't see one type of car that
~~~

was his style anywhere inside the warehouse.

"Find anything you like, young Warren?" Stevenson asked as he walked up beside Boss.

"You've got some nice wheels, but—!"

"Let me guess," Stevenson interrupted, "these are really not your types of cars, are they?"

"Pretty much!" Boss replied. "I'm more into Porsches, Ferraris, and Lamborghinis."

Stevenson nodded his head and smiled. He then looked across the warehouse to where Malcolm stood talking with Ike.

"Young Warren, you may not know this, but you're a lot like your father!"

"What's that supposed to mean?" Boss asked the man.

"All while your father and I were growing up, he was into fast and expensive cars and still is. He has a few of his own, but he only drives them when he's not working. But let me ask you something, ReSean," Stevenson said with a light laugh.

"What's up?"

"Do you consider yourself a businessman, or do you consider yourself a hustler?"

"Both!"

Stevenson smiled at the young man's answer.

"That was the perfect answer, young Warren! But let me let you in on something. It's good to be both a businessman as well as a hustler. But to be the perfect type of businessman, you must become more of a businessman but use the skills of a hustler when dealing with business decisions. You understand what I'm telling you, son?"

Boss slowly nodded his head and smiled at Stevenson. He then shifted his eyes around when they landed on a dark indigo, new-model Bentley GT Speed.

"What's up with the Bentley?" Boss said as he nodded toward the car.

Stevenson smiled at the young man's choice, and realized that he had understood his message perfectly.

"That's a perfect choice, young Warren! That car fits you!"

"Stevenson!" Malcolm called as he walked up to his son and best friend. "We've got a meeting in half an hour. You think we can get this finished up?"

"Let me get the room ready and find out what young Warren and his friends have decided to drive," Stevenson told Malcolm, winking at Boss and smiling as he turned and walked away.

"You find anything?" Malcolm asked Boss as soon as Stevenson walked off.

Boss nodded over at the new car he had picked out and said, "The Bentley over there next to the Audi RS7."

"Nice choice. It fits you!" Malcolm replied as he nodded his head, impressed.

~ ~ ~

Boss saw Stevenson's war room and picked out a shoulder holster for his Ruger and accepted a back holster for the chrome .40 caliber he was holding. Stevenson walked up with the back holster and told him it was his as a gift. Boss also accepted the hollow tips Stevenson passed out to him and the rest of the crew. Boss took Stevenson's cell and home phone numbers just as everyone was getting ready to leave. He was surprised when Stevenson hugged him, but he nodded after Stevenson had whispered in his ear.

"Where are the keys?" Trigger asked as he walked up to Boss. "Malcolm's got one of his boys taking my new ride back to the penthouse for me, so I'm driving with you. Up the keys!"

Boss shook his head and then tossed Trigger the new keys to the Bentley as he turned and walked around to the passenger side.

“Oh shit!” Trigger cried in shock. “Nigga, you picked a Bentley!”

“Come on!” Boss laughed as he climbed inside.

Chapter 19

BOSS STARED UP AT the glass high-rise office building from the passenger seat of his Bentley. He sat waiting until Trigger parked behind his father's Maybach. He then climbed out and began looking around the area. Boss turned and faced his father and Ike as Malcolm climbed out from the back of the Maybach, just as Black Widow and the others walked up on his right. Boss started walking toward his father as Malcolm began walking toward the building's front entrance.

"We're meeting Rachell Harris," Malcolm stated, speaking to Boss as the two of them walked side by side and headed in the direction of the elevator. "She's the widow of the late Donavon Harris, and she now has full control of the Harris business, but she knows less than she would admit she does."

"What's our business with her?" Boss questioned his father as he, Malcolm, Trigger, and Ike got onto the elevator while Black Widow, Savage, Joker, and Malcolm's four security men waited for the next elevator to arrive.

"We've agreed to combine our business with the Harris's, and then expand further than it is now!" Malcolm explained.

"So what's the catch?" Boss spoke up.

"She's having problems with Seven Hernandez," Malcolm said to his son with a smile.

Boss laughed lightly as he followed his father off the elevator. He began to ask another question but decided against it as he continued following Malcolm until they reached a tall, dark-wooded double door with two armed security guards on either side of it.

"Tell Mrs. Harris Malcolm Warren Sr. is out here!" Malcolm informed the guard on the right side of the door, to which he received a nod in return, before the guard turned and entered the office.

After they waited a little over three minutes, the door re-opened, and the guard motioned for them to come inside. Malcolm led Boss into the office, leaving Ike and Trigger out in the hallway to wait.

"Malcolm Warren!" Rachell Harris cried, smiling at the sight of him.

She quickly noticed the young man standing beside Malcolm, who was breathtakingly gorgeous.

"And who is this you've brought with you, Malcolm?"

"Rachell Harris, meet my son, ReSean Holmes,"

Malcolm introduced the two.

"ReSean Holmes," Rachell repeated his name while slowly looking over the unbelievably handsome young man. "It is really good to meet you, Mr. Holmes."

"Boss!" he stated as he slid his hands into his pockets.

"Excuse me?" Rachell asked.

"Call me Boss!" he told her. "It's what I'm known by, Mrs. Harris."

"Well I must ask that you call me Rachell then, Boss," she told him flirtatiously, smiling across the glass table. "Why don't you and Malcolm have a seat and we can talk."

After taking a seat across from Rachell at the twelve-seat glass table, Boss sat to his father's right as Malcolm spoke up first.

"So, Mrs. Harris, Last time we spoke you mentioned that you were willing to combine the two businesses and begin expanding."

"Yes, Malcolm. That is correct," Rachell told him. "I've also mentioned the problem that I've been—!"

"Seven Hernandez," Boss interjected, speaking up and drawing Malcolm's and Rachell's attention to him, and holding the green eyes of the dark-haired queenpin. "If there's an agreement between us, then you have no further reason to worry about this Seven Hernandez. I'll see to him myself!"

Rachell slowly smiled while staring directly at Boss.

"Malcolm, I think I may like this son better than the other one. He seems to be a man of business and getting things done!"

"I'm glad you approve, Rachell," Malcolm stated, cutting his eyes over to Boss, who sat calmly staring at Mrs. Harris.

~ ~ ~

After finishing up with Mrs. Harris and then attending a second meeting later that day, Malcolm took Boss and his crew on a bit of a sightseeing work tour of the city. He showed them various locations they controlled as well as other areas where they were conducting business with the other drug lords. Once they returned to the penthouse and stood out on the terrace, Boss asked his father the question that had been on his mind.

"You mentioned the others who we're supposedly dealing with as far as business goes, but who is it that we're having problems with? I do remember you saying we're here because you needed my help, so who's the problem?"

Malcolm remained quiet for a moment and then finally

answered his son.

"His name is Austin Jones, and he's been my major problem."

"Why?"

"Because it's like the others actually follow him, and he's backed up by Stephen King, who's major out here in Chicago."

"So answer something. How would this Stephen guy react if Austin turned up missing?"

"There'd likely to be a war!"

"What about the other way around?"

"You mean if Stephen King went missing?" Malcolm asked, looking to Boss and seeing his son nod his head in response. "Boy, you would first have to get close to King."

"You didn't answer my question!" Boss told his father.

"It'll probably be the same end result," Malcolm told Boss. "But if left to decide which to war against, it'll probably be Austin Jones."

Malcolm watched Boss stand up, nod his head, and look over the city. Malcolm was beginning to recognize the look that was on his son's face at the exact moment.

"What's up, ReSean? What's running through your head right now?"

"How much can you tell me about Stephen King?" Boss asked his father, ignoring Malcolm's question.

"What's Rachell's number?" Boss asked while pulling out his phone.

Malcolm grabbed onto his arm to get his attention. "ReSean, this isn't a game out here, and this isn't Miami. These muthafuckas don't play by the same rules!"

"I don't play at all!" Boss told his father, before he repeated his request. "What's Rachell's number?"

Malcolm shook his head and then provided Boss with Rachell's contact information for which he had asked.

~ ~ ~

Boss contacted Rachell Harris and agreed to meet with her at her mansion to gather information and to discuss Stephen King. Boss and Trigger left the penthouse and found Rachell's mansion after ten minutes of driving around the area of the address he was given. They drove up in Boss's new Bentley and were met by security at the front gate and allowed to drive through. After climbing out of the car, Boss was met by Trigger, who walked up beside him from around the driver's side. They were then met by more security at the front door of the two-story mansion.

"No disrespect, Mr. Holmes," the head of security and

Rachell Harris's personal bodyguard stated, "but, I'm going to have to pat both you and your friend down before you meet with Mrs. Harris."

Boss nodded his head and allowed the bodyguard to pat him down, removing both his Ruger and .40 caliber. Boss then looked over as the bodyguard removed Trigger's three bangers as well as his butterfly knife that he always kept on him.

"Right this way, Mr. Holmes!" the bodyguard stated, motioning Boss and Trigger up the steps to the front door.

Once they were inside the mansion, they continued to follow the bodyguard out onto a back patio, only to see Mrs. Harris lying out by the pool on a lounge chair in a two-piece bathing suit. Boss stopped behind the bodyguard as he announced his arrival.

Mrs. Harris set down her Dolce & Gabbana shades and smiled as she looked up to meet Boss's gorgeous eyes. She then motioned for him to sit down.

"Thank you!" Boss said, after taking a seat across from her.

"So tell me, Boss," Rachell began, smiling flirtatiously at him. "What is it you needed to speak privately about?"

"Stephen King!" Boss told her, watching the smile

slowly slip away from her lips. "What can you tell me about him?"

Rachell stared at Boss for a few moments.

"Boss, what's going on? Why are you looking to find out information concerning Stephen King?" she finally asked.

"I'll explain later," Boss told her. "What can you tell me?"

Rachell slowly shook her head before she began telling Boss everything she knew about Stephen King. Boss listened closely as Rachell told him what she knew about him. He learned that King was actually a lot more major than his father had painted him out to be.

"Whoa! You say that every Tuesday King takes his wife out to lunch at what restaurant?" Boss cut off Rachell.

"Supremely Divine!" Rachell told him. "It's one of four restaurants King bought for his wife."

"Supremely Divine, huh?" Boss repeated as he went into deep thought for a few moments, only to have those thoughts interrupted.

"Mom!" both Rachell and Boss heard someone call from the patio door.

"Demi!" Rachell said, smiling upon seeing her daughter. Rachell stood from her seat as Demi walked over and hugged her.

"I'm sorry," Demi said, after releasing her mother and noticing the two men sitting with her. "I didn't know you had company."

"We was just leaving!" Boss stated as he stood to his feet. "Rachell, can you text me the address to that restaurant, please. I'll then get in touch with you after our problem is taken care of."

Rachell nodded her head and watched as Boss and his friend walked off. She then looked over at her daughter.

"Mom, who is that?"

"ReSean Holmes!" Rachell told her daughter, smiling at the expression on her daughter's face. "He's the youngest son of Malcolm Warren."

"Wait!" Demi said, surprised at what she just heard her mother say. "You mean Malcolm Warren has another son?"

"That was him," Rachell said with a smile.

"Wow!" Demi said, smiling back at her mother. "He is gorgeous!"

"I thought so, and still think the same thing!" Rachell said as both she and her daughter began giggling.

~~~

Boss left Mrs. Harris's mansion and received the text
~~~

message with the address to Stephen King's wife's restaurant. Boss had Trigger find the restaurant and drive by it so he was able to get a look at the place and the area.

Once the two of them located the fancy and surprisingly large restaurant in a high-end neighborhood. Boss had Trigger drive by the place twice and then park two blocks down the street. Boss sat and checked out the restaurant and surroundings, taking in as many details as he could. He then looked up and down the two-way street entrance on which the restaurant directly sat.

"Let's go!" Boss finally said to Trigger while digging out his cell phone.

Boss first called Black Widow and told her that he and Trigger were on their way back to the penthouse and that he wanted everyone there. He then called his father.

"Yeah!"

"Pops, it's me! You busy?"

"What's up?"

"I need to holla at you about something, but not on the phone. You think you can swing by the penthouse tonight?"

"I'll be by at 8:00!"

"That'll work."

"Everything went good with Rachell?"

"Yeah! Everything went good," Boss replied. "I also met Rachell's daughter and was surprised that they look about the same age."

"Far from it though!"

"Yeah! I know!" Boss stated. "But I'ma let you go and catch you tonight."

"All right, Son."

After hanging up with his father, Boss was surprisingly still thinking about Rachell's daughter, seeing her face from memory. He shook off the thought and focused his mind back on business.

Chapter 20

VANITY SMILED AS SHE stood looking over the finishing touches of the strip club that was formerly the Pink Palace, but was now called The Empire. She looked over at Gigi as she walked up beside her.

"You did it again, girl!" Gigi told her, smiling as she also looked around the newly renovated strip club.

"Naw, girl!" Vanity said, still smiling as she looked back at her best friend. "Not me. We! We did it again!"

"Ummm, Vanity?"

Vanity heard her name and looked over toward her new assistant. "Yeah, Kelly? What's up?"

"Ummm, you have somebody out front who's here to speak with you," Kelly informed Vanity.

"Who is it?" Vanity asked, seeing the worried expression on the woman's face.

"I'm not sure who the woman is, but I recognized Malcolm Warren," she told Vanity.

"Father or son?" Gigi asked.

"Son!" her assistant replied.

Vanity looked over at Princess as she sat at the bar drinking an apple juice. Once Vanity caught Princess's eye, she stood up and headed Vanity's way.

"What's up, V?" Princess asked.

"Malcolm's here!" Gigi spoke up, before Vanity could say anything.

Princess whistled to get the attention of the security team that was put together for Vanity, and motioned them over.

"What you wanna do, V?" Princess asked.

Vanity sighed loudly and thought for a few moments. "Fuck it! Let me just straighten this out and be done with it!"

Princess motioned the guys toward the door ahead of Vanity. Princess then fell in step beside Vanity as they headed toward the front entrance of the club.

~ ~ ~

"Why the fuck are we waiting out here?" Brandi asked with a lot of attitude as she and Malcolm sat inside the backseat of his S550 Mercedes in the parking lot of The Empire.

"Brandi, just relax!" Malcolm paused, seeing the club doors swing open and a team of six men with guns in hand step outside.

They were followed by Vanity and three women. Malcolm also noticed the chrome .45 automatic in the hands of one of the women on Vanity's right side.

"Look at this bitch!" Brandi spit out, staring hatefully at Vanity through the tinted window of the Benz.

Malcolm shook off his stare, since he was still strongly attracted to Vanity. He then opened the back door and climbed out, followed by Brandi.

"Why am I not surprised!" Vanity said, giving Brandi a nasty look once she saw her step out of the Benz.

"Bitch, don't get—!"

"Vanity, you look good!" Malcolm said, cutting off Brandi.

He couldn't help but stare at Vanity in her silk Louis Vuitton pantsuit that fit her body perfectly.

"What do you want, Malcolm?" Vanity asked him. "I can't believe you're even here. Why are you even here?"

"To talk to you!" Malcolm replied as he started walking toward Vanity, only to pause when seven guns swung up aimed directly at him.

"You may wanna back the fuck up!" Princess spoke up, snatching out a twin chrome .45 and pointing it at Moses, who stood with his hand slowly creeping up to his waist. "Go ahead, big stupid! I got enough rounds to drop your big ass too. Stupid muthafucka!"

"So that's how it is between us now, Vanity?" Malcolm

asked, looking back at her.

"There is no us, Malcolm!" Vanity told him. "And you're lucky Boss isn't here right now, or there would be problems!"

"Fuck Boss!" Brandi yelled. "And fuck you, bitch! You think you're all that since Boss started messing with your nasty ass!"

"And I see you still wish you was me, huh, bitch!" Vanity stated with a smile.

Brandi started to rush toward her, only for Malcolm to grab her around her waist and stop her.

"I tell you what, Malcolm. I won't tell Boss about this visit, but my advice is to stay away from me and this club! I'm sure my man wouldn't like it that you've trespassed on what belongs to him. I can't say what or how he will react, even if you are his brother!" Vanity informed Malcolm.

Malcolm stared at Vanity a few minutes and felt his anger rising. He released Brandi and turned back to his car and climbed inside. Once they were inside the Benz and Moses drove away from the strip club, Malcolm stared out the window deep in thought, when Brandi interrupted.

"I can't stand that bitch! I wanna fuck that ho up so fucking bad that it drives me crazy!"

"Relax!" Malcolm calmly told her. "I think I have a way to make the both of us happy!"

~ ~ ~

Stephen King exited Supremely Divine with his wife, followed by their bodyguards. Stephen escorted his wife over to their diamond-black Rolls-Royce Ghost. Once inside, he allowed her to lean in and lay against his chest. Stephen then wrapped his arm around her and even kissed her forehead as their driver pulled off.

"Honey, I was thinking," Stephen heard his wife say, looking down at her as she lifted her head from his chest. He sat listening to her talk about them taking a trip somewhere away from Chicago to just relax and spend some time together.

"I tell you—!"

Brrrrrrr! Brrrrrrr!

"Oh my God!" Melody King screamed as both she and Stephen heard the semi-automatic machine guns go off.

Stephen instinctively pushed his wife low as he pulled out his .38 from his side holster. He looked out the back window and saw the craziness as his driver was doing one hell of a job getting him and his wife away from the scene unharmed.

Once the driver slowed the car but was still driving at a good speed, Stephen King helped his wife up and then put away his gun.

"Sweetheart, are you alright?"

"Stephen, where are we?" Melody looked over and asked while nodding her head.

Stephen also looked around but didn't recognize the area. He was just about to call up to the driver, when the car suddenly stopped in the middle of a dark road.

"What the hell!" Stephen called out, when he heard the car locks activate.

~ ~ ~

Boss watched from the backseat of his Bentley with Rachell seated next to him while Joker climbed out and walked away from the Rolls-Royce Ghost. Boss then saw Black Widow and Savage appear out of the darkness.

"You may want to watch this!" Boss said to Rachell, pointing over in the direction of the Rolls-Royce.

Rachell followed Boss's instructions, and began to smile once the woman and muscular man began filling the Rolls-Royce with bullets from their MAC-11 and AK-47.

Boss looked over at Rachell and saw the smile on her face. He called up front to Trigger and motioned for him to drive as he focused back on Rachell.

"So now that that's over, are you still questioning my father's and my ability to build this business, or are you with us fully?"

"Lead the way, Boss!" Rachell told him, realizing that Chicago really had a problem on its hands with ReSean Holmes a.k.a. Boss.

To be continued . . .

Text Good2Go at 31996 to receive new release updates via text message.

BOOKS BY GOOD2GO AUTHORS

SLUMPED
PART 1
JASON BRENT

SILK
WHITE
STRANDED

TEARS
HUSTLER

TEARS
HUSTLER
2
SILK WHITE

GOOD 2 GO PUBLISHING PRESENTS
TEARS
OF A
HUSTLER
3
SILK WHITE

TEARS
OF A
HUSTLER
4
YOU'VE BEEN WARNED
SILK WHITE

SILKWHITE
TEARS
OF A
HUSTLER
5
THE SPADES

GOOD 2 GO PUBLISHING PRESENTS
SILKWHITE
TEARS
OF A
HUSTLER
6

THE
TEFLON
QUEEN
SILK WHITE

THE
TEFLON
QUEEN
2
SILK WHITE

THE
TEFLON
QUEEN 3
HARD TO KILL
SILK WHITE

THE
TEFLON
QUEEN 4
MR. DEATH
SILK WHITE

GOOD 2 GO PUBLISHING PRESENTS
THE
TEFLON
QUEEN 5
DEEP COVER
SILK WHITE

GOOD 2 GO PUBLISHING PRESENTS
THE
TEFLON
QUEEN
NO MERCY
SILK WHITE

GOOD 2 GO PUBLISHING PRESENTS
THE PANTY
RIPPER
REALITY WAY

GOOD 2 GO PUBLISHING PRESENTS
THE PANTY
RIPPER
REALITY WAY

GOOD 2 GO PUBLISHING PRESENTS
TIED TO A
BOSS
J.L. ROSE

GOOD 2 GO PUBLISHING PRESENTS
TIME
IS
Money
SILK WHITE

Young
Goonz
REALITY WAY

THE HACKMAN
NOW AVAILABLE ON YOUTUBE!

FILMS

To order books, please fill out the order form below:

To order films please go to www.good2gofilms.com

Name:____

Address:____

City: ________________ State: ______ Zip Code: _________________________________

Phone:____

Email:____

Method of Payment: Check VISA MASTERCARD

Credit Card#:____

Name as it appears on card: ____

Signature: ____

Item Name	Price	Qty	Amount
48 Hours to Die – Silk White	$14.99		
A Hustler's Dream - Ernest Morris	$14.99		
A Hustler's Dream 2 - Ernest Morris	$14.99		
Bloody Mayhem Down South	$14.99		
Business Is Business – Silk White	$14.99		
Business Is Business 2 – Silk White	$14.99		
Business Is Business 3 – Silk White	$14.99		
Childhood Sweethearts – Jacob Spears	$14.99		
Childhood Sweethearts 2 – Jacob Spears	$14.99		
Childhood Sweethearts 3 - Jacob Spears	$14.99		
Childhood Sweethearts 4 - Jacob Spears	$14.99		
Connected To The Plug – Dwan Marquis Williams	$14.99		
Connected To The Plug 2 – Dwan Marquis Williams	$14.99		
Flipping Numbers – Ernest Morris	$14.99		
Flipping Numbers 2 – Ernest Morris	$14.99		
He Loves Me, He Loves You Not - Mychea	$14.99		
He Loves Me, He Loves You Not 2 - Mychea	$14.99		
He Loves Me, He Loves You Not 3 - Mychea	$14.99		
He Loves Me, He Loves You Not 4 – Mychea	$14.99		
He Loves Me, He Loves You Not 5 – Mychea	$14.99		
Lord of My Land – Jay Morrison	$14.99		
Lost and Turned Out – Ernest Morris	$14.99		
Married To Da Streets – Silk White	$14.99		
M.E.R.C. - Make Every Rep Count Health and Fitness	$14.99		
My Besties – Asia Hill	$14.99		
My Besties 2 – Asia Hill	$14.99		
My Besties 3 – Asia Hill	$14.99		
My Besties 4 – Asia Hill	$14.99		
My Boyfriend's Wife - Mychea	$14.99		

My Boyfriend's Wife 2 – Mychea	$14.99		
My Brothers Envy – J. L. Rose	$14.99		
My Brothers Envy 2 – J. L. Rose	$14.99		
Naughty Housewives – Ernest Morris	$14.99		
Naughty Housewives 2 – Ernest Morris	$14.99		
Naughty Housewives 3 – Ernest Morris	$14.99		
Naughty Housewives 4 – Ernest Morris	$14.99		
Never Be The Same – Silk White	$14.99		
Stranded – Silk White	$14.99		
Slumped – Jason Brent	$14.99		
Supreme & Justice – Ernest Morris	$14.99		
Tears of a Hustler - Silk White	$14.99		
Tears of a Hustler 2 - Silk White	$14.99		
Tears of a Hustler 3 - Silk White	$14.99		
Tears of a Hustler 4- Silk White	$14.99		
Tears of a Hustler 5 – Silk White	$14.99		
Tears of a Hustler 6 – Silk White	$14.99		
The Panty Ripper - Reality Way	$14.99		
The Panty Ripper 3 – Reality Way	$14.99		
The Solution – Jay Morrison	$14.99		
The Teflon Queen – Silk White	$14.99		
The Teflon Queen 2 – Silk White	$14.99		
The Teflon Queen 3 – Silk White	$14.99		
The Teflon Queen 4 – Silk White	$14.99		
The Teflon Queen 5 – Silk White	$14.99		
The Teflon Queen 6 - Silk White	$14.99		
The Vacation – Silk White	$14.99		
Tied To A Boss - J.L. Rose	$14.99		
Tied To A Boss 2 - J.L. Rose	$14.99		
Tied To A Boss 3 - J.L. Rose	$14.99		
Tied To A Boss 4 - J.L. Rose	$14.99		
Tied To A Boss 5 - J.L. Rose	$14.99		
Time Is Money - Silk White	$14.99		
Two Mask One Heart – Jacob Spears and Trayvon Jackson	$14.99		
Two Mask One Heart 2 – Jacob Spears and Trayvon Jackson	$14.99		
Two Mask One Heart 3 – Jacob Spears and Trayvon Jackson	$14.99		
Wrong Place Wrong Time	$14.99		
Young Goonz – Reality Way	$14.99		

Subtotal:			
Tax:			
Shipping (Free) U.S. Media Mail:			
Total:			

Make Checks Payable To:
Good2Go Publishing
7311 W Glass Lane,
Laveen, AZ 85339

CPSIA information can be obtained
at www.ICGtesting.com
Printed in the USA
LVHW090905260419
615550LV00013BA/599/P

9 781947 340015